There was more going on here than just a simple detective trying to cut her teeth on her first murder case, he thought. This case meant something to the woman and he intended to find out just what it was.

But he could also see that he wasn't about to get it out of her by pressuring her or bombarding her with questions at this point. This would take finesse—and patience.

If the woman wound up hanging around that long.

As he came up to the door to the medical examiner's offices, he paused with his hand on the doorknob.

"Something wrong?" Liberty asked him when he made no move to go in.

"Just making sure you're up to this," Campbell told her. "First times are hard."

"This isn't my first time," Liberty informed him.

He smiled at her, sending shockwaves all through her system. "Just making sure."

She resented his inference. She didn't like being a lightning rod for someone's concern. It made her feel fragile and those days were permanently behind her.

Or they were supposed to be.

Dear Reader,

Liberty Lawrence was an orphan from her very first memory. For the first eighteen years of her life she was passed around in the foster care system, and for purposes of self-preservation she never allowed herself to form any sort of attachments with any of those people. When Florence, a registered head nurse, took her in, the woman was determined to get through to Liberty. It was because of Florence that Liberty got her BA and a degree in criminology, and eventually went into law enforcement. It seemed ironic that the only person who ever cared about Liberty was murdered by a serial killer. The case eventually went cold, but Liberty never gave up on it.

When a new case surfaces with the same MO in Aurora, California, Liberty takes what vacation time she has amassed and goes to see if the detective who caught the case in Aurora has any leads.

And so begins an unlikely partnership...and a chance at love with Campbell Cavanaugh.

I hope you enjoy reading about Liberty's journey and transformation half as much as I enjoyed writing about it. Thank you for reading one of my stories and as always, from the bottom of my heart, I wish you someone to love who loves you back.

With thanks,

Marie Ferrarella

CAVANAUGH JUSTICE: SERIAL AFFAIR

Marie Ferrarella

Recycling programs for this product may not exist in your area.

ISBN-13: 978-1-335-75970-2

Cavanaugh Justice: Serial Affair

For questions and comments about the quality of this book, please contact us at CustomerService@Harlequin.com.

Harlequin Enterprises ULC
22 Adelaide St. West, 41st Floor
Toronto, Ontario M5H 4E3, Canada
www.Harlequin.com

Printed in U.S.A.

USA TODAY bestselling and RITA® Award–winning author **Marie Ferrarella** has written over three hundred books for Harlequin, some under the name Marie Nicole. Her romances are beloved by fans worldwide. Visit her website, marieferrarella.com.

Books by Marie Ferrarella

Harlequin Romantic Suspense

Cavanaugh Justice

Cavanaugh's Bodyguard
Cavanaugh Fortune
How to Seduce a Cavanaugh
Cavanaugh or Death
Cavanaugh Cold Case
Cavanaugh in the Rough
Cavanaugh on Call
Cavanaugh Encounter
Cavanaugh Vanguard
Cavanaugh Cowboy
Cavanaugh's Missing Person
Cavanaugh Stakeout
Cavanaugh in Plain Sight
Cavanaugh Justice: The Baby Trail
Cavanaugh Justice: Serial Affair

The Coltons of Colorado

Colton's Pursuit of Justice

Visit the Author Profile page at Harlequin.com for more titles.

This Book Is Lovingly Dedicated

To The Most Important

People In the World to Me:

My Family:

Charlie, Jessica, Nicholas,

Melany, Logan

And my brothers,

Michael and Mark

Without You There Is Nothing

Prologue

At first, Liberty didn't even realize that the murders were connected. It was a matter of not seeing the forest for the trees—until she suddenly began comparing notes.

Calhoun, Arizona, wasn't exactly a big town. The population numbered less than a thousand even during the times when it was "booming," and the town wasn't thought to be booming for a while now. However, what Calhoun had always been was a nice, peaceful, law-abiding town right from the very beginning.

Or at least that was what Liberty had believed until she'd begun to compare notes and notice things that had escaped her attention before.

For the first tumultuous eighteen years of her life,

the young woman who was to become Detective Liberty Lawrence had lived an altogether different, nomadic life.

Abandoned almost from the moment she was born, Liberty had never had a place she could call home and was, quite frankly, on the path to self-destruction—until Florence Bishop had come into her life.

Florence had been a forty-five-year-old head nurse working in the ER when Liberty had been brought in looking as if she had beaten and abused to within an inch of her life. The tough-talking sixteen-year-old orphan had rejected any and all pity. All she'd wanted to do was to leave the site of her humiliation and possibly find a way to retaliate against her newest foster mother who had done this to her.

Despite Liberty's attempts to push her away, Florence had seen something in the angry young orphan and immediately opened her heart to her.

Even though Liberty had fought her at every turn, Florence decided to take her in as a foster mother, consequently providing the rebellious teenager with the only real home she had ever known.

It wasn't an instant alliance and definitely not all sunshine and roses. It had taken Liberty a while before she let even *some* of her barriers down. Although she never said the words out loud, Liberty was eventually very grateful to the sharp-featured nurse for taking her into her home and for making sure that she went to school even as she rebelled against any show of authority.

There was no doubt about it in Liberty's mind.

Florence brought out the best in her; a "best" Liberty hadn't even been aware of having until Florence had taken her in hand.

It was because of Florence's efforts that Liberty had graduated high school and then gone on to get a college degree. And it was because of Florence, Liberty finally told the woman during what turned out to be their last visit, that she actually *had* a life.

Things at that point had looked as if they were finally on the right track.

And then tragedy struck.

Less than three weeks later, Florence's body had been found lying in the alley behind the hospital where she worked. The nurse had been strangled.

Liberty had been beyond devastated.

By that time Liberty had worked her way up to being the small police department's only other detective, and she was determined to find Florence's killer. At the time of the murder, she had absolutely no experience in murder cases—Calhoun wasn't exactly a place that had any sort of a body count. Despite that, Liberty threw herself into working the case every chance she could for the next few months. Come hell or high water, she was determined to find her foster mother's killer.

It was during this time she discovered that Florence was not the killer's first victim.

Or his second.

The more Liberty looked into the cases, studying similar ones in the southwest area, the more she discovered. She found that this was not just an ordinary killer. This was a serial killer. A serial killer with, it eventually turned out, a high body count.

In total, there were thirty victims spread out across small towns in Arizona, New Mexico and Nevada. The cases all had a few things in common. The victims were all nurses over the age of twenty-five and under the age of fifty. They each had also all been strangled with piano wire.

Becoming almost obsessed with finding the killer, Liberty investigated as much as she possibly could while still doing her regular day-to-day job at the police station.

And now the latest victim had just turned up in Aurora, California.

That meant that the killer was getting bolder because, looking up information about the most recent place that a killing had taken place, she found that Aurora had a much bigger police force than any of the other towns where the killer had struck.

Was the killer getting more brazen, or was there another reason for this sudden switch in venue?

The more research she did, the more confident Liberty became that she could get someone interested in the fact that all of these murders had been the work of a serial killer.

Her own chief, Elliott Atwater, had just expressed relief that the killer no longer appeared to be roaming their streets, but had evidently moved on. Atwater confessed he hoped that life could get back to normal.

But for Liberty, life would never get back to even *close* to normal until she could finally achieve closure. And closure would only come once the killer was captured and stopped.

The only way that was going to happen, Liberty decided, was if she took some time off and followed this latest trail to the killer's most recent killing site: Aurora, California.

Making up her mind, Liberty walked into Atwater's small office and announced, "I'm going to take my vacation now, Chief."

The chief looked up from his morning coffee. He didn't look surprised. "It's that serial case of yours, isn't it?"

Liberty saw no reason to pretend otherwise. He had always been good to her, if somewhat too lax in his methods for her taste.

"It is," she replied.

Atwater paused to examine his records. "Well, since you're not that big on taking vacations, you've got a total of three weeks amassed." Because she was the youngest on his force, he apparently felt it behooved him to warn her. "But if you wind up taking any longer," the chief told her, "you might not have a job to come back to."

Being a detective was very important to Liberty. It finally felt as if she fit in somewhere. But finding Florence's killer was worth every sacrifice. She owed the woman a huge debt she would never be able to even begin to repay.

"I understand, sir," she told the chief. "And I'm willing to take my chances."

Elliot Atwater merely shook his head. He didn't

want the young woman taking chances, although he knew she would. He had come to learn that Liberty was exceptionally stubborn once she set her mind to something.

"Stay safe, Liberty," the chief ordered her. "I don't want to lose my best detective."

Her mind was already making plans for her trip to Aurora and she was only half listening. "Don't worry, Chief, you won't. I fully intend to remain safe," Liberty promised the older man, her partial mentor, with feeling.

The chief almost believed her.

Chapter 1

The anger was finally beginning to fade.

But then, it usually did right after one of his eruptions. And this flare-up had really felt like a major one. So much so that it felt as if it would never pass.

But, eventually, it did.

Exhaling a long breath, he glanced at his watch to see how long it had taken this time. He never managed to keep track while it was going on—predominantly because he couldn't.

The anger and rage that had shot through him, causing such damage as it vibrated within him, left him on the very brink of oblivion until it was all finally over with.

The last time it had happened, it had taken over

twelve hours for him to emerge and come up for "air" again.

Someday he knew he probably wouldn't emerge. But "someday" wasn't now, and that was all he was concerned about.

Now.

All he could remember when one of these eruptions hit was an overwhelming wave of white heat.

And anger.

Lots and lots of anger.

When it was finally over, he would always find himself standing in an entirely different place than before.

And she was dead.

Again.

The problem was she never stayed dead. Oh, she tried to fool him. She would take on different voices, different features, different hairstyles and color, but it was *always* her.

Always.

She couldn't begin to really fool him.

She had *never* been able to fool him. Evil had a certain kind of look about it, and no matter what, it always came through. Sometimes it just took longer, but it couldn't remain hidden indefinitely.

She couldn't remain hidden indefinitely.

This time, he left the body where it had fallen. Hidden in the weeds.

It was time to get back to his life again and finally put Sarah behind him where she belonged.

Until she emerged again the next time.

* * *

"Hey, Cam, there's someone out here to see you," Campbell Cavanaugh's partner, Brandon Choi, called out as he crossed the squad room floor to reach Campbell's desk.

Brandon found he had to put his hand against his partner's chest to keep the man from shooting out of the room like a launched missile.

Detective Campbell Cavanaugh was a man who was obviously on a mission.

The next minute, he said as much. "Do me a favor," Cam requested. "I'm planning on getting a head start on Christmas shopping this year. *You* see this guy for me."

Brandon frowned, momentarily sidetracked. "Christmas shopping? Forgive me if I'm wrong, but isn't this just the beginning of December? You don't usually get rolling until the second week of December is over. And, besides, I thought you and that lady friend of yours broke up and became history a while back ago. Is there someone new in your life you haven't told me about?" Brandon studied the man whose ability to attract women without any effort had made him envious, despite the fact that Choi was happily married himself.

Campbell shrugged off the question. "It never hurts to be prepared," he told his partner. "Besides, I do have other people to buy gifts for," he pointed out. "The people in my family could populate a small town as it is. I learned my lesson last year when I wound up forgetting Jacqui, my own sister. This year I'm bringing a checklist so nobody gets left out."

"Well, look at you being all conscientious and everything," Choi marveled with a laugh. "Personally, I don't know how you manage to keep track of your family. Hell knows I couldn't."

He wanted to get going. "So you'll talk to this guy, whoever he is?" Campbell asked as he started to walk out of the room.

"Well, number one, I would, but Susan might get *really* jealous," he said, referring to his wife of less than two years. "And number two, this isn't a guy," Choi added.

Campbell raised an eyebrow, his interest clearly piqued. "Oh?"

"Yeah," his partner replied, grinning. "Definitely 'oh.'"

Despite Campbell's reputation as an appreciator of lovely-looking women—a street that ran both ways—the homicide detective was not the type to be easily fooled or led astray, no matter how beautiful the woman promised to be. Beauty alone was not enough to sustain Campbell's interest—but it certainly was enough to capture it for a short while.

Campbell looked at his partner suspiciously. Something didn't seem quite right about this. "Okay, what's the catch?"

"No catch, partner. The woman is here on business," Choi informed him.

But Campbell wasn't buying it. Something was

up—or maybe he had just been on the force too long and had grown too suspicious.

"What sort of business?" He wanted to know.

Choi merely smiled again at his partner in response. "Tell you what, why don't you ask her?"

"Because I'm asking you," Campbell pointed out. His green eyes met his partner's. "I'd rather not have any surprises."

Choi's wide grin seemed to almost say, *Yes, you do.* His smile grew even wider. "Sorry, partner, can't help you there."

All thoughts of getting a jumpstart on his holiday shopping—he was a sucker for Christmas, always had been—was pushed into the background. This person who had come looking to talk to him had captured his attention—but not to the exclusion of everything else.

"Try," Campbell stressed, his eyes pinning his partner in place.

"Okay, but you're taking all the fun out of this," Choi told him more seriously, "She's a detective out of Calhoun, Arizona—"

"Where?" Campbell asked. To his recollection, he had never heard of Calhoun, Arizona.

"Calhoun," Choi repeated. "From what I gather, it's more or less a hole-in-the-wall in Arizona."

"Okay." Campbell nodded, accepting that for now. "And why is she here?"

"It seems that case you caught the other day when I went in to fix my broken tooth..." Brandon began to explain.

"Okay, what about it?" Campbell pressed.

"Well, according to the detective, your case bears a lot of similarities to one of hers," Choi told him. "The upshot is that she would like to talk to you about it."

"If that's the case, why were you grinning?" Campbell asked. He still wasn't fully convinced that this wasn't some sort of a prank on Choi's part, or that he wasn't dealing with misinformation. Otherwise, why would a detective from a tiny town in Arizona come all the way out here, looking to talk to him?

"Maybe she's just passionate about her work. You'd have to see her to understand," Choi explained then added, "Trust me on this."

Now his curiosity was definitely aroused. Campbell sat back down at his desk.

"Okay," Campbell told the other man, "why don't you bring her in?"

His partner nodded, obviously pleased. "I'll be right back," Choi promised.

Campbell barely had time to contemplate his partner's strange behavior before Brandon Choi returned. And, as promised, he wasn't alone. In front of him, he was ushering a very shapely young blonde into the room.

So this, Campbell thought, had to be the detective from Calhoun, Arizona. He was instantly interested and totally captivated.

"Sorry about the tight spaces," Choi said to the blond detective, apparently intrigued by her hair in one thick braid down her back. Belatedly, he waved his hand at the disarrayed room. "Our squad room really needed to get a facelift and the powers that be decided to do it just before Christmas—and also before, according to them, the rates are supposed to go up. Be careful not to walk into anything," he warned, appearing ready to catch her if that proved necessary. "You'll either get paint smeared on your clothes or wind up tripping."

"Thank you, Detective Choi," the attractive young woman said, "but I learned how to walk a long time ago."

From the look on Choi's face, Campbell decided he had no idea what to expect. The visitor was either going to be the type to bring a cold shiver racing up and down his spine—or a very warm one.

After listening to her speak, it seemed as if it was definitely going to be the latter.

"Mystery solved," Campbell murmured to himself as he belatedly got to his feet.

Liberty was certain that she heard the other detective say something and she eyed the tall, broad-shouldered, dark-haired man.

"Excuse me?" she asked. "What did you just say about mysteries?"

She really is a knockout, he caught himself thinking. Coming to, Campbell found his tongue. "That I liked solving them," he answered after a beat.

Liberty looked at him a little curiously, not quite sure what to make of him, then finally said, "Nice to know," although she thought it a rather odd comment for the detective to make.

"I'm Detective Campbell Cavanaugh," Cam said by way of introduction, putting his hand out to the visiting detective. “I take it that you’ve already met my partner, Detective Brandon Choi.” He nodded at the man standing next to her.

“Yes, I did,” the blonde confirmed.

Not exactly a great conversationalist, Campbell mused when nothing more followed that sentence.

“And you are?” he prodded, waiting for the woman to tell him her name.

“Detective Liberty Lawrence,” she answered.

Campbell caught himself smiling at the name. “Very lyrical.”

The young woman shrugged carelessly. “I suppose,” she murmured.

She was still standing, Campbell realized. He strove to make her feel a little more comfortable, as well as hoping to get her to relax. He sincerely doubted that he could make her feel *less* comfortable even if he tried.

“Why don’t you sit down?” Campbell finally invited, gesturing toward the chair that was facing his desk.

The detective from Arizona looked at the chair he pointed to as if she weren’t all that comfortable about sitting in it. They exchanged glances in silence before she finally gave in and did as the detective suggested.

Liberty sat on the very edge of the chair, looking as if she was ready to spring to her feet at any second.

Campbell looked at Choi, whose expression was definitely not illuminating. Campbell took the lead, finally saying, “My partner here tells me that you have a case that’s similar to ours.”

"Not 'similar' to yours," Liberty corrected him. "*Exactly* like yours. As a matter of fact," she continued, "at last count, I discovered that there were thirty murder victims altogether, including the one you just found, all exactly like yours."

"You discovered all the bodies?" Cam asked. It was obvious that he didn't believe this detective from the little Arizona hole-in-the-wall town.

"No, I didn't find them," she informed Campbell, a trace of annoyance in her voice because he was obviously being condescending. "I just counted them. Other detectives found the bodies. A lot of other detectives," she emphasized. "But no one connected the cases until I started putting things together and seeing the similarities. The murders were all obviously committed by the same serial killer."

The woman was coming on a little strong for his tastes, Campbell thought. Detectives this obsessed usually missed a lot of things just to make their theories fit the crime they were looking into.

"Are you sure about that?" Campbell asked the woman, studying her.

There was not a second's hesitation on her part. "Absolutely," Liberty answered.

"So, Detective Liberty—" Campbell began but got no further.

"It's Detective Lawrence," she corrected the detective then reluctantly told the man, "or you can call me Liberty if that makes you feel more comfortable talking to me."

The look on her face fairly dared him to resort to using her first name.

Which was why he did.

"All right, *Liberty*," Campbell began gamely, "what makes you think those thirty bodies you've collected—"

"Cases I reviewed," Liberty said, correcting him once again.

"'Reviewed,'" Campbell amended with a nod of his head. "Just what makes you think this is all the work of the same killer?" he asked.

Obviously she was going to have to lead this horse to water, Liberty thought. But this was extremely important to her—not to mention the latest victim—and she wanted a chance to see the evidence as soon as possible.

"Number one," Liberty enumerated, "all the victims were nurses between the ages of twenty-five and fifty. Number two, every one of them was strangled using piano wire. And, number three, all the bodies were discarded in the alley somewhere close to the hospital where they worked—if not directly *by* the hospital where they worked. The killer was obviously recreating something," she concluded.

Campbell thought for a moment then said, "Certainly looks that way." His tone was less distant than it had been a moment ago. He raised liquid green eyes—eyes that mirrored the eyes of most of the men in his family—to Liberty's face. Inclining his head, he told the detective, "I apologize."

The apology took her aback. She wasn't accustomed to someone apologizing to her. Usually, when she turned out to be right—and she often was—whoever had disagreed with her just backed off and the matter was dropped.

It was always far better just to back away.

But Liberty wasn't after accolades—she never was. What she wanted to do was to right a wrong. In this case, the wrong required bringing the killer to justice—once she was able to find the killer.

The next piece of the puzzle as far as she was concerned. But this detective had just completely thrown her with his apology.

"I don't understand," Liberty said, still confused. "Just what are you apologizing for?"

"For sounding as if I was discounting what you were saying," Campbell confessed quite honestly. "It sounded as if you were filling in empty spaces, making the evidence fit your pattern of the crime. But apparently it turns out that you were right. In this case, the pieces of the puzzle are exactly as simple as they seem."

She nodded her head. "We just need to find how all these people came in contact with the killer. And why these particular women and not other women."

"Simple questions," Campbell agreed. "But not such simple answers. Why are you so caught up in this?" He wanted to know.

"I don't like murder," she said evasively, not about to explain to him about Florence. For one thing, dealing with the investigation was a conflict of interest since one of the victims was someone she cared about.

Someone she was determined to avenge. She didn't want to just hand this detective any ammunition to use against her.

"Most homicide detectives don't," Campbell said, commenting on the fact that she'd said she hated murderers. "But that still doesn't explain why you followed this trail of breadcrumbs to another state."

Liberty's eyebrows drew together. She didn't care for being challenged—or interrogated. "I had no idea I had to submit an essay written in triplicate."

"You don't," he told her mildly. "Where's your partner?"

"I don't have a partner," she told him.

"Something happen to him—or her?" Cam asked. Or was it a case of her being too difficult to work with? he wondered.

"Yes. Availability. Calhoun is a very small town. I'm the only detective they have at the moment. The other one retired and wasn't replaced. It's not as if we have a lot of murders to follow up on. Now, if you're satisfied, I want to ask you a few questions before I leave or you get called away."

Cam nodded as he leaned back in his chair, never taking his eyes away from hers. She had the lightest blue eyes he had ever seen.

"Go ahead," he urged. "Ask away."

Chapter 2

"Actually," Campbell interjected, "before we get started, I've got some questions of my own for you."

She knew what he was going to ask. "I'm doing this on my own time. I took all of my accrued vacation so I could do some independent investigation into the various victims. Anything else you want to ask me?"

That sounded pretty ambitious from where he was sitting, not to mention that she sounded rather defensive. But if he was going to get involved in this, he needed things to be crystal clear.

"You said there were thirty victims in all that you knew of," he said.

"Yes?" Liberty asked guardedly.

"Would you happen to have a list of those names?" Campbell asked.

For the first time since she had met him, she found herself smiling. He'd thought he was going to corner her—but he wasn't.

"Funny you should ask," she told him. The next moment, Liberty took out a folded piece of paper from her purse. Opening it up, she held the paper out for his benefit.

What Campbell noticed first was the *way* the names were written. The woman's handwriting was exemplary. He didn't come across that too often these days.

Looking up at her, Campbell made a calculated guess. "Parochial school?"

"Foster system," she answered crisply. Seeing the surprised look on his face, she decided to explain. "There's not all that much you can do by way of entertaining yourself when you're in the system. Me, I practiced my handwriting because it was something that wasn't done anymore and it didn't cost anything, just paper and a pen."

Because she had momentarily gotten excited about finally getting somewhere with the case and had admitted way too much to this good-looking stranger, Liberty immediately withdrew.

"Now, if we're through playing Twenty Questions about my life, I'd like to get back to focusing on these cases. Has the autopsy on your victim been done yet?"

"As a matter of fact, she's probably almost finishing up by now—or at least, it's on her schedule,"

Campbell told the visiting detective. "You really seem eager." He couldn't help noticing. "Let me guess. This is your first murder case, isn't it?"

She wasn't about to fall into that trap again. "Something like that," she told him vaguely.

"'Something like that'?" he repeated, puzzled by her terminology. "It either is or it isn't." When he paused, the detective from Arizona didn't add anything, so he decided to prod. "Okay, which is it?"

"Why is that so important to you?"

"Just trying to get an idea of who I'm working with," he answered.

"Okay. Then you first," she said, turning the tables on the glib detective.

"All right," he told her good-naturedly. "I'm the fifth-born kid in a seven-sibling family and, before you ask, yes, we're all cops. As are most of my cousins," he added. It was a fact he took for granted, but he reminded himself that there were still people who didn't know that.

"Just how many cousins do you have?"

His beaming smile seemed to radiate from every part of him. Had she just stumbled onto an inside joke? She couldn't tell. "You remember that small town you mentioned that you came from?"

Her guard was instantly up. "What about it?"

He noticed the expression on her face but, for now, he let it go. "Well, those cousins I just mentioned? They could have easily populated it."

"You're exaggerating, right?" she asked warily.

He merely smiled at her. "Just ask anyone here

about the Cavanaughs," he told her. "You'll find out if I'm exaggerating or not."

For the time being, Liberty gave him the benefit of the doubt. "That big, huh?"

Campbell's smile simply grew wider. He had to admit that the glimmer in her eyes just got to him.

"That big," he told her without any fanfare and then changed the subject. "Look, I think the ME who's currently on duty is my cousin-in-law Kristin. If she's finished with the autopsy, I could call in a favor."

These Cavanaughs were everywhere, weren't they? she silently marveled. "What kind of a favor?"

"I could ask her to speed up writing the preliminary draft of the report so she could get it into my—*our* hands," the detective corrected.

Okay, this was almost too much to absorb, Liberty reasoned. Was this family actually *everywhere*? "Let me get this straight," Liberty enunciated slowly. "You're telling me that you're related to the ME, too?"

"To one of them, yes."

"Oh, just one of them?" Liberty asked sarcastically, not sure if she actually believed this detective or not. What he was telling her didn't seem possible.

"Don't be a wise guy," Campbell told her, cutting through whatever rhetoric was about to follow. "I'm offering you a chance to get in on this while it appears to still be in the works," he pointed out. After all, she was the one who'd approached him, not the other way around. "If it is what you're telling me it is, it sounds like, once the news gets out, all hell is going to break loose and you might have trouble getting close to it. Now, are you interested or not?" he asked her even though he had more than a hunch that he knew full well what her answer was going to be.

Liberty frowned. She didn't like coming off as being so needy, but this did involve Florence and she owed the woman more than she could ever possibly say. Consequently, Liberty was forced to make an admission she would have never made otherwise. Certainly not willingly.

"Oh, I'm interested," she told the detective then emphasized, "Definitely interested."

And if for some reason it turned out that this detective was playing her, Liberty thought, she made a silent promise that she would find a way to make him pay for it.

Big-time.

"Then let's go," Cam was saying as he stood from his desk.

"Right now?" she asked, hoping he wasn't trying to lead her on just to "change" his mind at the very last minute.

"No time like the present," he told her pleasantly. "Unless you've decided to change your mind."

"Not me," she told him firmly. Gathering her things together, she slipped them back into her purse. "Just where is this morgue? I'll get my car and follow you."

"No need for that," he answered.

"I'd rather go in my own car," she said firmly, cutting in. That way, she felt she would have control over where she was going. Control meant a great deal to Liberty. It had ever since she'd been old enough to understand what that entailed.

Campbell inclined his head as he led the way out of the squad room. "Have it your way," he told her. "But it might be kind of tough getting your car into the elevator."

Liberty stopped walking and stared at the detective. "Come again?"

If possible, his smile grew even larger. "The morgue is located in the basement," he told her. "We moved it into the police station a while back to make accessing the morgue more efficient. It eliminates traveling back and forth between destinations in order to view the body and to talk to the medical examiner. This way, everything's all in one place."

Why did she get this feeling that this sexy detective was gloating, or talking down to her?

"You have a point," Liberty conceded.

"You sound surprised," he noted, overlooking her frosty tone as he pressed for the elevator.

She supposed that maybe the man was trying his best to be helpful. "Actually," she admitted, "I am. I don't usually associate efficiency with a big-city police department."

For a second, she'd lost him. "You mean Aurora?" he asked.

"Yes, I mean Aurora," she answered. Maybe she'd been too quick to offer praise, she thought. "What did you think I meant?"

He shrugged. "I guess I still think of Aurora the way most of the old-timers do."

"Old-timers?" she questioned. He couldn't be referring to himself. "You're what? In your twenties?"

"It's not a matter of age," Campbell clarified. "It's a state of mind passed on from my parents. From a lot of parents who came out here to live, back in the day." He could see that she wasn't following him, so he explained further. "Aurora was initially a small town that just kept taking baby steps and growing. It never really stopped growing, but be that as it may, it still retained that small town feel to it."

Campbell considered his words. "I guess that's what makes it so unique and keeps the people here hanging around," he told her.

The elevator car arrived at their floor and opened its doors. Campbell waited for this visiting detective to get on before following her in. When he finally got on, he pressed for the basement.

"You sound like a former tour guide," Liberty commented.

"No," Campbell told her. "I'm just a citizen who loves his hometown." He let his answer sink in before he added, "That's why I decided to join the police department."

She filled in the blanks. "Because you like being in a position of authority?"

"No," he told her. "Because I like preserving the peace and making sure that the people who live here are safe."

That sounded far too noble, she thought. And then

she looked at him. The detective was perfectly serious. "You mean that, don't you?" she asked Campbell as the elevator came to a stop.

While he was used to questioning things as a detective, the way he viewed things as a person was an entirely different matter.

"I wouldn't say it if I didn't," Campbell said simply. He gestured to the open elevator doors. "I believe this is our stop."

Stepping out of the elevator, Liberty looked down the long hallway. She was surprised to find that it was brightly lit. Her own precinct believed in saving on electricity.

Campbell saw the look on her face and offered a guess. "Were you expecting to find a darkened dungeon?"

"Calhoun doesn't have an official morgue. We have to use the county morgue that's located in Madison."

"Going on a field trip to view the body of the deceased can't be a fun excursion," Campbell commented as he led the way to the offices used by the medical examiner.

Liberty couldn't help thinking back. Not to when she'd had to view the nurse who had been the killer's latest victim, but to when she'd had to go to identify her foster mother's body.

For just one harrowing moment, she felt a cold chill down her spine, alternating with a flash of overwhelming heat. The sensation effectively paralyzed Liberty until she was finally able to draw air back into her lungs.

She realized that they had stopped walking and that the too-handsome-for-his-own-good detective was watching her. There was concern in his eyes. "Are you all right?"

"I'm fine," Liberty answered him all too quickly.

"You don't look fine," he said. "You want to sit down or have something to drink? Water? The computer lab's right over this way." He pointed toward another door. "I'm sure they won't mind if you stop to—"

"I said I'm fine," she told him more sharply. She shrugged. "I just get a little claustrophobic when I'm underground."

He nodded as if he believed her, making her feel worse. "Why don't you go back upstairs and wait in the squad room?" Cam suggested. "I can get the report and bring it to you when it's ready."

"That's all right," she told him dismissively. "It passed."

He looked at her more closely. It was obvious that he didn't believe her. "You sure?"

"I said it passed," Liberty said curtly.

He stood there looking at a woman who was trying his patience. "Has anyone ever told you that you make it difficult to be nice to you?" Campbell asked.

Liberty tossed her head. "It's been mentioned," she answered. The moment she did, she regretted snapping at the detective. "I'm sorry. But I am over it," she added when she saw that he was waiting for something further.

"It?" he questioned, trying to get to the bottom of

what was really bothering her rather than just accept some made-up excuse. He was a Cavanaugh and Cavanaughs liked to get to the bottom of things. Not out of some morbid curiosity, but because it made them see things more clearly.

At least, that was the excuse he used, he thought, and it did have validity.

A thought occurred to him. "Were you the one who found the body?" he asked her.

Liberty avoided his eyes. It wasn't something that she wanted to get into, especially not with a stranger. "Not exactly."

"Then what 'exactly'?" Campbell asked.

She shrugged. "Viewing the body just reminded me of something," she said evasively.

"Can I ask what?" Campbell inquired in a lowered voice.

"You can ask," Liberty responded.

Campbell studied her. He had faced enough stubborn family members to be very familiar with the look that was currently on her face. "But you're not going to tell me, are you?"

A partial smile broke through. "You catch on fast, Cavanaugh."

"I have to," he admitted. "There's a lot of competition in my family." He knew he wasn't going to get anything out of her on the subject, at least not today. "Well," he told her, "I'm here if you decide you need a sympathetic shoulder to lean on."

"I'll keep that in mind," she said crisply, doing her best to bury his offer the moment it was tendered.

"You do that," he told her.

There was more going on here than just a simple detective trying to cut her teeth on her first murder case, he thought. This case meant something to the woman and he intended to find out just what it was.

But he could also see that he wasn't about to get anything out of her by pressuring her or bombarding her with questions at this point. This would take finesse—and patience.

If the woman wound up hanging around that long.

As he came to the door that opened into the medical examiner's offices, he paused with his hand on the doorknob.

"Something wrong?" Liberty asked him when he made no move to go in.

"Just making sure you're up to this," Campbell told her. "First times are hard."

"This isn't my first time," Liberty informed him.

He smiled at her, sending shockwaves all through her system. "Just making sure."

She resented his inference. She didn't like being a lightning rod for someone's concern. It made her feel fragile, and those days were permanently behind her.

Or they were supposed to be.

"Don't you have a sister or a cousin to take care of instead of me?" she asked, trying to redirect the detective's attention to someone or at least some*thing* other than her.

"Not at the moment," Campbell answered.

Turning the doorknob, he opened the door then gestured inside. “All right, let’s go,” he said.

To Liberty, it sounded almost like a battle cry.

Chapter 3

Dr. Kristin Alberghetti Cavanaugh had just untied her face mask, lowering it. It still hung at half mast around her neck, its blue color matching the scrubs she wore whenever she performed an autopsy. She had met Malloy, the man she was destined to marry, while performing wholesale autopsies on bodies uncovered beneath an out-of-the-way cacti nursery.

Kristin maintained that if all those unexpected bodies hadn't caught her off guard, then nothing ever would.

But Kristin had to admit that she was shaken up this time. She had just discovered, after having conducted the autopsy, that the body she'd just worked on was one of the many, according to the woman she had just met, that had been left by a prolific serial killer. That had rattled her to the core.

Kristin nodded at her husband's cousin, but her attention was drawn to the young woman he had brought into the morgue with him.

"Hi. I hear that our latest murder victim brought you in all the way from Arizona," Kristin said, smiling at Liberty.

"Calhoun, Arizona," Campbell specified, knowing that Kristin liked details whenever possible.

Hearing the name, Kristin shook her head. "Sorry, I'm not familiar with that name," the medical examiner apologized.

"Don't worry about it. Not many people are," Liberty told her. Her eyes were drawn to the body on the table. "Is that the victim?" she asked. Without thinking, she had automatically lowered her voice out of respect for the deceased.

"It is," Campbell confirmed. And then, to lighten the mood, the detective quipped, "They frown on the lab assistants taking naps on the tables when it's slow."

"Don't pay any attention to Cam," Kristin told the woman from Arizona. "Yes, to confirm what Campbell just said, that is the latest victim." She watched as the blonde who had come in with Campbell slowly approached the table, circled it, looking at the body from all angles and studying the woman. There was a very strange expression on the detective's face. "Did you know her?" Kristin asked.

"No, not her," Liberty answered, only half paying attention to what the medical examiner had just asked her.

"But you knew one of the killer's victims, didn't you?" Campbell guessed, going with his gut reaction.

The detective's words sank in belatedly and Liberty's eyes darted to his face when she realized what he was saying. She inadvertently stiffened just a little.

"Why would you say that?" she asked defensively.

"Call it 'copley intuition.'" Campbell told her in all seriousness.

"'Copley'?" Kristin repeated with a laugh. "Well, that's a new one on me," she confessed.

"Calling it intuition sounds a lot better than a 'gut' feeling," Campbell told the two women.

"Maybe," Kristin agreed. "But 'copley'?" The medical examiner shook her head, showing how she felt about the strange term. "I really don't know about that. Is that even a word?"

The corners of Campbell's mouth curved. "I'll work on it," he promised glibly. "So," he said, addressing the ME more seriously, "is this victim similar to the others?"

"According to the reports I reviewed earlier, right down to the grade of piano wire the killer used," Kristin answered. It was obvious by the way the medical examiner spoke that she had divorced herself from the actual deed being investigated. Otherwise, she would have had difficulty remaining removed as she performed these autopsies.

Liberty studied the deceased more closely. "Was death immediate?"

The detective from Arizona might have seemed removed, Campbell thought, but something in how she asked about the deceased told him that this was personal to the investigator.

"If you're asking me if she suffered," Kristin said, "I don't think she did. There are no defensive wounds on the victim, indicating that the killer caught her by surprise. And then the piano wire did the rest."

"That's a relief," Liberty murmured then added, "That she didn't suffer. It means that the killer wasn't doing this in order to watch the victim suffer and plead with him for her life."

"Campbell mentioned that you said the victims were similar," Kristin told Liberty, interested in gathering as much information about the case as possible for her notes.

Liberty nodded. "All the victims so far have been nurses," she told the doctor. "And they were between the ages of twenty-five and fifty."

"No other similarities?" Kristin asked. "Hair color, eye color, weight?" She ticked off each item, watching Liberty's face as she mentioned it.

Liberty thought, doing a quick mental review of the victims she had compiled. She shook her head. "Nothing else except for the piano wire—and they were all Caucasian."

Kristin glanced at Campbell then asked the visiting detective, "Why do you think the killer would use piano wire?"

"My guess is that it probably has something to do with the original murder victim," Campbell answered, keeping one eye on Liberty to see if she agreed or had something contradictory to add. "Maybe the first person he killed this way was his mother or some other female relative who happened to be a nurse who also either taught music on the side or forced the killer to practice the piano as a boy. You'd be surprised what idiosyncrasies—"

"You said that *all* the victims were nurses?" Kristin asked. She found herself being drawn into particulars of this case.

"So far, they have been," Liberty verified.

"Maybe they also taught music. Say, on the side?" Campbell suggested, searching for a way to connect the two things.

"Good question," Liberty responded. "I don't know, but that will definitely be one of the questions I intend to ask."

"Are you planning on tracking down the victims' families and interviewing them?" Campbell asked. Considering that there were thirty victims, it sounded like a very ambitious undertaking to him. She was going to need help.

"If I can find them," Liberty acknowledged. "If I can't, then I'll try to find anyone who knew the victim and talk to them to get some kind of insight."

This was beginning to sound more like an obsession than just a case. "How long did you say you plan on taking off?" Campbell asked.

"Three weeks." Liberty had a hunch that she knew what he had to be thinking. "But if I feel like I'm getting somewhere, I can try to get an extension," she added.

"Out of sheer curiosity, how many people do you have working with you?" he asked. "I know you mentioned that you were the only detective in Calhoun, but do you have any assistance, or police officers helping you go through these cases?"

She hated being put on the spot or admitting that there wasn't anyone to turn as she worked this investigation.

"It's not about the number of people I have," Liberty replied.

It wasn't hard to read between the lines, Campbell thought. "So it's just you," he guessed.

Liberty raised her chin. "Sometimes it just takes one person," she said defensively.

The detective smiled at her. "In a perfect world, maybe. But then, in a perfect world, these kinds of things don't happen," he concluded philosophically.

Was he goading her, or was he just having fun at her expense? Eithcr way, shc didn't take kindly to it. "Is there a point to this?" she asked him.

"Well, the key point is that this investigation you're proposing to spearhead would go a lot faster if you had help."

She certainly couldn't argue with that, even though she would have wanted to, especially since she felt as if this detective was deliberately pressing her buttons to get a reaction out of her.

"I'll put an ad to that effect in the local paper when I get home," Liberty told him.

"No need to do that," Campbell said. He made it sound as if he had some sort of a solution to her situation.

"Oh? Well, I'm open to any suggestions," she said glibly then added, "*Decent* suggestions." The look in her eyes challenged him. "All right, so what's *your* idea?"

He smiled, sensing that she wouldn't like this, but then, if she was all alone in this, she really didn't have much choice, did she?

"Well, I've got some time coming to me," Campbell told her.

Liberty frowned, totally forgetting about the medical examiner in the room for the moment. "And what good does that do me?"

She also didn't care for the amused smile that curved the detective's lips—never mind just *how* appealing that smile made him look.

"Not much for adding two and two together, are you?" Campbell asked her.

Kristin cleared her throat, temporarily drawing their attention away from one another. "Not that it isn't fascinating watching the two of you spar, but I do have work to get to. I can have a rough draft of this report in your hands within an hour or so. Until then, maybe you can take this outside?" she suggested brightly, looking from one to the other.

"Sorry, Kris," Campbell apologized, giving her cheek a quick, affectionate kiss. "I'll be on my best behavior when I come back to get the report," he promised with a wink.

As he began to leave, he realized that the woman he had brought in with him still hadn't made a move to follow him. She had remained standing next to the medical examiner.

"Um, Arizona?" he said, waiting to get her attention so that she would leave with him.

Instead, Liberty looked almost sheepishly at Kristin. Maybe she did need to apologize. "I'm sorry, Doctor. I don't usually allow myself to get carried away like this. It's just that you were right," she admitted. "This *is* a very special case for me. And not just because of this latest case—" she nodded at the body on the table "—or the one that I caught in Calhoun, even though murder in Calhoun is a very rare occurrence. We don't exactly have murderers in town, much less serial killers."

Kristin nodded. "I understand perfectly."

This was where she walked away, Liberty silently reminded herself. She had smoothed out the feathers that she had ruffled—or at the very least, the feathers appeared to be smoothed out.

Despite that, Liberty continued to stand where she was. She needed these people's cooperation and it appeared that the detective was willing to pitch in even after she had become so prickly. The very thing that had her being so closemouthed when she was around the chief and his people back in Calhoun now had her willing to open herself up to this detective and the medical examiner.

She really didn't have a choice in the matter.

"Actually," Liberty began, her eyes sweeping over

the medical examiner and then over toward Campbell, "you don't."

Kristin appeared to be at a loss as to whether or not to press Liberty for any further details, but Campbell had no such misgivings. "All right, then why don't you explain it to us?"

Liberty pressed her lips together, carefully weighing her words. "It's personal," she finally responded to Campbell.

"Are you talking about the case or the explanation?" Campbell asked.

Liberty took in a deep breath before answering, telling him, "Both."

That was still rather ambiguous as far as Campbell was concerned. "Why don't you tell us about one or the other to start with?"

She might as well give him some of the background, Liberty decided, even though part of her really wished she hadn't started out on this path to begin with. But she had, and she did owe him for being willing to help.

"I didn't tell anyone in Calhoun that the case was personal for me because, as a rule, I wouldn't be allowed to investigate a case that was personal, even though it actually is part of a larger case involving a serial killer."

"No argument so far," Campbell told her, nodding his head. He could feel Kristin looking at him, which stopped him. "What?"

"You know perfectly well *what*," the medical examiner told him, then looked at Liberty and began to explain what was actually behind her comment. "There have been more than a few members in the family who have either looked the other way or hoped the authorities in charge would wind up looking the other way when they, the members, took up an investigation that was close to them.

"Cavanaughs," she continued, "you'll find out, aren't exactly married to the rules when those rules manage to get in the way of their solving a crime."

Liberty flashed a smile at the medical examiner, surprised that the doctor was willing to admit that to her.

"Well, that's good to know," the visiting detective acknowledged.

Campbell decided to dive in.

"You were saying before Kristin interjected her sidebar?" he asked, waiting for Liberty to continue and to hopefully give him the answer to the question he had asked when she'd first come to him with this case.

"I said that the case was personal," she repeated, still attempting to find the right words to explain her dilemma.

"Yes, I got that part," Campbell assured her.

His eyes met hers and this time, he wasn't struck by how very blue they were. He was struck by the sadness he saw there.

"Was the person who was killed by this serial killer someone in your family?" Kristin asked.

"I don't have a family," Liberty answered automatically. "I never did." Even after all this time, the words still tasted bitter on her tongue.

And then she pressed her lips together, pushing on. "But Florence was the closest person I ever had to a family and I owe it to her to find the worthless excuse for a human being who did this to her."

"Florence," Campbell repeated. "That was one of the names on that list you showed me."

It wasn't a guess.

Despite herself, Liberty was impressed. "There were thirty names on that list."

"He's blessed with one of those memories," Kristin told her.

"You mean photographic?" Liberty asked. "That must come in handy in your line of work."

"Not exactly photographic," Campbell corrected. "But it's the next best thing. I remember things. I just have to see it written once or hear it said, and it's pretty much sealed in."

"I guess I'd better watch what I say around you, then," Liberty said half seriously.

"Only if you decide to lie, because then it'll trip you up. Otherwise," Campbell said with a grin, "you have nothing to worry about."

"What I just said about this being personal..." she began.

Campbell could guess where she was going with this. "Sorry, I wasn't listening."

Kristin smiled. "That's his way of saying don't worry. But you two really have to make yourself scarce now—unless you don't want this report."

"We're gone, Kris," Campbell assured her, opening the door.

Liberty preceded him out. She was more than eager to hold the report in her hand.

Chapter 4

"I take it that you've already notified Cynthia Ellery's next of kin?" Liberty asked as they walked out of the medical examiner's office.

"Actually, we've just managed to locate the victim's next of kin late yesterday," Campbell told her. "Her sister, Judith, was away on vacation. When we reached her, she said she would be getting back into town today."

A very cold chill ran up and down Liberty's spine. "Does she know what she's coming back to?" Liberty couldn't help asking. The situation brought back so many of her own memories of when she'd found out about her foster mother's murder.

"She guessed before I could tell her," Campbell admitted.

The answer surprised Liberty. "She *guessed* that her sister was dead? Doesn't that strike you as being a little odd?" she asked Campbell. "If someone called me about my sister, my first guess wouldn't be that you were calling because she was dead."

Something just wasn't making sense to Liberty. Could the woman's sister have had anything to do with Cynthia's murder?

"When I identified myself as being part of the police department, she immediately thought I was calling to notify her that something had happened to Cynthia, like a car accident," Campbell said.

Liberty rolled that explanation over in her mind. "Well, I suppose that does make more sense," she responded.

Campbell nodded. "I had to tell her why I was calling."

Liberty recalled that she had had so many questions of her own once the shock of her foster mother's death had had time to register.

The elevator arrived and they got on. "But you are going to follow up, on your phone call, right?" she asked the detective. "You're not just going to leave it at just a phone notification."

"Sounds like you already know the answer to that one," Campbell replied.

"Let's just say I was hoping that you wouldn't disappoint me." She turned her face up to his. "Would it be all right if I tagged along? And no, I don't know the answer to that question, but I'm hoping that you won't say no."

Liberty couldn't read the expression that passed over Campbell's face and, for a moment, she found herself suspended in limbo, her mind scrambling to come up with a way to convince the detective, if he did turn her down, that she would be an asset if she were allowed to come along.

Campbell took pity on her and put her out of her misery. "First of all, it would be rather cruel of me to tell you that you couldn't come along when I talk to the victim's relative after you came all this way to inform me that there were more victims. Second, I would be lying if I said that I couldn't use the backup. These notifications can become very uncomfortable and get rather sticky. Having a woman come along might make the victim's sister feel marginally better. So yes, you can definitely come along."

Liberty had to admit that she was surprised, as well as relieved, that it wound up being so easy.

"Thank you. Frankly, I was bracing myself for a fight," she admitted.

"Well, I'm glad I could disappoint you," he said with a laugh. "Unless, of course, you're the type who thrives on confrontations and arguments."

"No, not usually," she told him as the elevator came to a stop on the first floor. "But if you're wondering, I don't run away from them, either."

Campbell laughed, his smile managing to set up residency in her chest despite Liberty's best efforts to block her reaction to this man. He had a smile that somehow managed to undulate through her entire system.

"Can't say that surprises me," he told her. Campbell began to make his way to the building's front exit. "So, unless you've decided that you have something else to turn your attention to—"

"Not at this very moment," she told him a bit too emphatically.

"Then let's go pay Cynthia Ellery's sister a visit," he said, secretly grateful he wouldn't be facing the ordeal alone. It wasn't that he shirked his responsibilities or would even put them off, but he had always felt that there was emotional safety in numbers. "All right. I'll drive."

Liberty had no problem with that and wondered if he was expecting her to argue with him over the arrangement. "It's your town and you know your way around,"

"It's my *city*," he corrected. "But yes, I do. My car's parked right over here in the rear lot." Campbell pointed it out for her benefit, leading the way to a brand-new, fully loaded silver sedan.

Liberty let out a low, appreciative whistle. The car was a fine-looking piece of machinery.

"I guess they must pay detectives really well in Aurora," she commented.

For a split second, Campbell didn't know what she was referring to and then he realized why she had said what she had. He wasn't all that into cars.

"Oh, you mean the car," he proclaimed. "The department just replaced my old car. They had to," he confessed. "I was really very partial to my previous vehicle until the driver of the car I was pursuing decided to make a sudden U-turn and tried to flatten it so that I wouldn't wind up taking him in."

She could vividly picture that confrontation. "Were you hurt?" Liberty asked.

A quick scan of the man showed her that he didn't seem to have a scratch on him. Was he lucky, or was he just putting her on?

"Actually, I wasn't. But the car really was," he said sadly. "I managed to jump out of the car and get out of the way just in time—except for this." He pointed to a thin, long scratch along his neck.

"Oh, ouch," Liberty said, sucking in a breath. She hadn't seen the mark before because it was on the side that she hadn't been facing—until he had just pointed it out.

Campbell laughed under his breath. "That wasn't exactly quite the word I used at the time, but yes, 'ouch,'" he agreed.

"And you said that your car was totaled?" Liberty asked him.

The memory of that incident was still very vivid to him. "Yes, it was."

"I guess you're lucky that nothing worse happened."

That wasn't exactly the way he viewed it. "Well, I consider losing a car pretty bad," he told her.

She looked at his vehicle skeptically. Maybe driving it bothered him. A little like a bad memory he couldn't get rid of.

"Would you like me to drive?" Liberty offered. "My vehicle isn't nearly as pretty, but it is reliable."

He wasn't sure why she was making the offer. "The accident wasn't my fault."

"I never said it was." She told him the first thing that came to mind. "I just thought you might like a break and I could drive."

"As you pointed out, this is my city and I know where I'm going," he told her. He had no idea where she could have gotten the idea that he might want a break from driving.

"You could give me directions," she said. Her lips curved ever so slightly. "I'm sure you're very good at telling people where to go."

"Why, Arizona, did you just make a joke?" Campbell asked with a laugh.

"No, just an observation," she answered. "And why do you keep calling me Arizona?" Liberty asked. After all, he did know her name.

"That's where you're from, isn't it?" he asked, starting up the car after she had buckled up. "And you have to admit that it sounds better than calling you Calhoun," he added with a grin.

"Why would you have to call me any of that? Did you forget my name?" she asked, assuming that was the only reason he had for falling back on calling her by the state she had initially come from.

"Well, you don't much look like a 'Lawrence,'" he said.

Her brow furrowed as she tried to make sense out of what he was saying. "But I look like an 'Arizona' to you?"

"Yes." When she looked at him quizzically, he explained. "It's the smell of wind in your hair. Makes me think of Arizona," he said, adding, "I visited there once. Tucson, specifically. Ever been?"

"Not that I recall," Liberty answered evasively. Actually, she had been to Tucson. She had been to several cities in Arizona, none of which she really cared to remember. That was back during the time when she'd found herself being passed from one foster home to another, fitting in nowhere and longing to be old enough to be on her own. Tucson was one of the places she'd run away from in her effort to be independent because she'd felt that no one had earned the right to take control of her life.

Not until Florence had come along and taken her in hand.

Liberty banished the memory out of her thoughts for the time being. Being nostalgic wasn't going to find Florence's killer or bring him to justice, she reminded herself.

Campbell noticed that the detective had lapsed into silence and couldn't help wondering if something he had said had struck a nerve.

It didn't take long for Campbell to bring them to their destination. He pulled up in front of a tidy, one-story home and parked by the curb.

"You ready?" he asked Liberty.

She sighed, looking at the small house and thinking of the person who lived there. Nothing was ever going to be the same once they talked with her.

"Is anyone ever ready to shatter someone else's world?" Liberty asked.

Maybe this was a bad idea, Campbell thought. "She's already been informed about her sister's death. And you don't have to come if it makes you uncomfortable."

"Yes, I do," Liberty insisted. It was her duty. "And my comfort has nothing to do with it."

He studied her face, unable to make up his mind about this woman. "Are you always so difficult to deal with?"

"'Difficult'?" Liberty repeated in genuine surprise. "And here I thought I was being easygoing."

Campbell shook his head.

"Think again," he told her, but Liberty noted that there was an amused smile on his face.

Getting out, Campbell circled around to the front passenger side and opened the door for her before she had the chance to.

Liberty continued to sit where she was, staring at him as Campbell held the door for her. "What are you doing?"

"I thought that was rather obvious. I'm holding the door open for you. Hasn't anyone ever held open the door for you, Arizona?" he asked.

As far as she knew, she was the very picture of independence. "Why would they want to?" Liberty questioned.

His eyes met hers. "You know, before you go back to that little town of yours, Arizona, you and I are going to have to have a long talk."

"Yeah, we'll see," Liberty said without committing to anything. She got out of the vehicle.

Campbell noticed the way she was looking around as they went up the front walkway. It made him think of a wistful kid, which had him wondering about the woman who was accompanying him. If she remained in Aurora for those three weeks she had mentioned, he promised himself that he would get her to talk about how she had arrived at this point in her life—and what she had experienced prior to that. Maybe that would be construed as meddling, but he was a Cavanaugh. Good or bad, it was a family trait.

He had a feeling that she had gone through a lot of experiences, good and bad, that had made her the woman she had become.

Maybe he was wrong, Campbell thought—but he had a sneaking suspicion that he wasn't.

Liberty had just assumed that the detective with her was rather laidback, but then she saw him squaring his shoulders just a fraction of a second before he rang the doorbell.

Maybe he wasn't as blasé as he was attempting to portray.

It made her feel better about the man. He was genuine.

When no one came to the door, Campbell rang the bell again.

"Maybe you got the time wrong," Liberty suggested. "Or Cynthia's sister decided she wasn't up to talking to the police just yet."

Campbell frowned. "The longer she puts it off,

the worse it's going to get for her." He knew that for a fact.

He was about to ring the bell a third time when the front door finally swung open. The woman in the doorway was a startling sight to see.

Judith Ellery's face was all puffy and swollen, like someone who had been crying for the better part of the day, which she obviously had.

The victim's sister looked almost bewildered when she eyed the couple standing on her front doorstep.

To set the woman's mind at ease, Campbell immediately took out his wallet and badge.

"I'm Detective Campbell Cavanaugh," he told the grieving woman, introducing himself. "I believe we spoke earlier on the phone." He put his identification away and nodded toward Liberty. "This is Detective Lawrence. She's from Arizona, and is consulting with me on this case." Glancing past the woman's shoulder, he could see that she was alone. "We would like to ask you some questions, if it's all right with you?"

"All right with me?" the woman echoed almost incomprehensively. "Nothing is ever going to be all right again," she lamented as she tried to hold back a fresh wave of sobs.

Judith Ellery held up her hand to stop the detective from saying anything further until she could get herself under control again.

"Can I get you some water to drink?" Liberty asked, taking the lead and surprising Campbell.

The victim's sister pressed her lips together, shook

her head and then swallowed before taking in a deep breath.

"No, that's all right," Judith told the two detectives standing in her doorway. "Just give me a minute," she requested, still struggling to regain control over herself.

"Take all the time you need," Campbell told her kindly.

Fresh tears were sliding down the woman's shallow cheeks, taking the very same path they already had previously.

Judith's voice was shaky as she spoke. "I warned her, you know. I told Cynthia that if she wasn't careful, something bad would happen to her. But she just laughed at me, told me she was a 'big girl' and that if she could take care of all those patients who came into the ER, she could certainly take care of herself in the outside world."

Tear-filled eyes looked from one detective to the other. "But she couldn't, could she?" Judith asked, her emotion-filled voice cracking.

"What did she mean by that?" Campbell asked. "'Take care of herself in the outside world'?" He wanted to know, repeating the words the victim's sister had just used.

"She was talking about those stupid dating sites," Judith angrily snapped. "You know, those anonymous ones where you make arrangements to meet up with men who could be Jack the Ripper for all you knew." Judith began to sob again. "I warned her this could happen. I *warned* her. But she wouldn't listen to me. She always acted as if she knew better than me."

Judith looked at the detectives with tear-swollen eyes. "But she didn't, did she? Damn it, why couldn't I make her listen?" she sobbed.

Chapter 5

So, the victim was in contact with a dating service. It was definitely an avenue to explore, Liberty silently decided.

She made a mental note to look into whether any of the other serial killer's victims had availed themselves of dating sites. At least it was a place where she could start.

"Would you happen to know any of the names of the men your sister met with?" Campbell asked the woman before Liberty had a chance to do the same. "Or maybe the name of the site she used?"

At the very least, they could try to get the necessary information from the dating site, as long as they explained the situation and promised to keep the investigation a secret, Campbell thought. Granted, it was a long shot, but it just might work.

However, Judith shook her head. "I really don't know any of that," she confessed. "Cynthia knew I didn't approve of her using sites like that, so she didn't talk about it with me. She might have mentioned something about it to some of her friends at the hospital. From what I gathered, they all thought the same way she did. Except they're still alive."

Judith pressed her lips together as she paused for a moment. Tears were getting the better of her again. She let out a deep, emotional breath. "I told her there was nothing wrong with meeting men the old-fashioned way, but she wouldn't listen to me. And now she's gone." Judith's voice broke again.

"'The old-fashioned way,'" Campbell repeated. "And that was…?" His voice trailed off as he waited for the victim's sister to complete the sentence.

"Through her place of work, and church," Judith answered. She wiped away her tears. "I met my late husband that way. He was a teller at the same bank that I was. But Cynthia said she didn't want to have her choices limited like that." More tears began to stream down the woman's face. "And now she has no choices at all," Judith sobbed and then covered her face with her hands. "Oh, lord, I wish she had listened to me. Cynthia would still be alive now if she had." Judith sounded as if her heart was literally breaking.

Liberty exchanged glances with the detective at her side. They couldn't just leave the woman in this condition.

Putting her arm around Judith's shoulders to comfort the distraught woman, Liberty asked, "Is there anyone we can call for you? Maybe a friend? Or another relative?"

Judith waved away the question. "I have someone I can call," she finally answered, her voice throbbing with emotion. "I'll be all right," she assured the two detectives with her.

"Well, if it's all the same to you," Campbell told the woman, "we'll wait until they get here. We wouldn't feel right leaving you alone like this." The statement was apparently directed toward Liberty, since the victim's sister had her head down, struggling to get control over her emotions.

Detective Cavanaugh's stock went up considerably in Liberty's estimation and she nodded her agreement with his statement.

Meanwhile, Judith deferred Campbell's offer, saying, "You don't have to." But the pitiful smile she offered both of them said far more than her words.

The detectives wound up staying with the victim's sister until her friend showed up—which turned out to be within the hour. When the woman, Angie, came on the scene, Campbell quickly explained the situation to her in its entirety. Judith's friend vacillated between shock and sympathy.

Campbell left both women with his business card and told them not to hesitate calling him if they remembered anything pertinent, even the smallest thing.

"Think it's someone that Cynthia met on a dating

site?" Liberty asked Campbell as they left the victim sister's house.

Campbell shrugged. "It's as good a possibility as any, I guess. At least it's a place to start. Starting a murder investigation is a lot like being confronted with a thousand-piece puzzle. You dump out all the pieces on the floor—wondering how in the hell all the pieces are going to fit together—and then you realize that at least five of those pieces were left out of the box.

"But you can't let that get to you," he told her as they got into his car. "You just keep working the pieces until they finally somehow all fit together."

"Is that how you view the investigation?" she asked Cam. "I've got to say, that description is kind of daunting."

"If it were easy, there would be a lot more investigators to go around instead of dropping out," Campbell told her. "What do you say we go to the hospital and see if we can find some of Cynthia's friends? Maybe at least one of them knows what dating site she used."

Liberty nodded. "I was just going to suggest that," she told Campbell.

"Great minds think alike," Campbell said, flashing her a smile.

Liberty looked at him with suspicion. "Are you making fun of me?"

He glanced at her as he turned the corner. Why would she even think that?

"No, I'm not," Campbell told Liberty. "That was

supposed to be a compliment. You know, you're going to have to learn how to tell the difference. For one thing, not everything is meant to be an insult or taken to be fighting words."

He was right, she thought. She was too quick to take offense. She would have to tone that down.

"Sorry," she murmured.

"Don't be sorry," he told her. He didn't want her apologies, he wanted to be able to work with her. "Just learn how to relax a little."

"Right. Relax," she mocked. "While investigating a serial killer."

She was definitely making fun of him now. But Campbell decided to take it in stride. He told her what his uncle, the chief of detectives, had told him when he'd first came to work on the police force.

"If you don't find some humor, however small or inane, to hang on to, in the long run, you're going to wind up losing your sense of humanity."

"What is that, something from a fortune cookie?" Liberty asked him.

"No, from Chief of Detectives Brian Cavanaugh," Campbell answered mildly.

Color shot into her cheeks. She had certainly put her foot into it that time, she thought. "I didn't mean to insult anyone..." she began.

Campbell's smile was meant to reassure her. "You didn't. The Chief of D's has a very thick hide—and a very decent sense of humor," he added with a wink just as he pulled into the Aurora Memorial Hospital's front parking lot.

Cynthia Ellery had been an ER nurse for the last five years, so the ER on the first floor was their first stop.

"I guess they've all heard the news by now," Liberty commented, looking around at the staff populating the general area.

It was obvious that the murder of one of their own had deeply affected a great many of the nurses and orderlies, as well as the doctors who were currently on duty during this shift.

Asking around, Campbell and Liberty had no trouble locating people who not only knew the late victim, but had nothing but kind words to say about Cynthia Ellery.

But as far as knowing anything personal about the nurse that might help them in the investigation, that unfortunately turned out to be an entirely different story.

The detectives kept coming up against dead ends time after time.

"Well, I knew she was single, but that's about it. She was a great nurse, though. And she was always willing to fill in in a pinch no matter how long a shift she had put in," the head nurse on the floor told them.

"I didn't even know she was looking to get fixed up," another nurse told them when they questioned her about her association with Cynthia.

"If I'd known, I would have introduced her to my cousin, Joe. He's not exactly a catch, but he's a good man with a big heart," yet another nurse volunteered.

Over and over again, they heard the same responses to their questions. Everyone knew Cynthia, but no one really seemed to *know* her.

In the end, although it took some doing, they did find a nurse who'd known that Cynthia was looking for a match on a dating site ironically named *Finding the Right One.*

"Would you happen to know if she used her real name when she signed up?"

"Oh, I know she did," the nurse, Abby, told them. "I can't say if the guy she went out with did. She saw him several times, though. Always at a restaurant. Cynthia was a hopeless romantic, but she wasn't stupid."

Liberty crossed her fingers. "Would you happen to know which restaurants she went to in order to meet this guy?"

"I know that she went to the Blue Hawaiian, but as far as the other restaurants she went to—" The woman lifted her shoulders in a hapless shrug then let them fall again. "I'm sorry. If she told me, I don't remember. We're usually very busy here in the ER."

"Don't worry about it," Campbell told her. "Anything you can tell us, anything at all, will be helpful."

The nurse shook her head, embarrassed. "I'm drawing a blank," she confessed. "It's like my brain froze."

"Well, if it happens to unfreeze," Campbell said, giving her his card, "please give me a call."

"Well, we didn't exactly strike out," Campbell told Liberty, sensing that she might need a little bit of a pep talk to bolster her confidence after they walked away. "We've got the name of a dating site plus a restaurant. Maybe someone at the restaurant might remember seeing her—and with whom."

It was obvious that their next stop was going to be the Blue Hawaiian restaurant.

But in the end, before they left the hospital, it was an orderly who supplied them with at least some of the answers.

The orderly, Luis Montenegro, a short, thin man who had a habit of blending into the background, overheard them talking as they were about to leave the ER.

"Are you two investigating what happened to Cynthia Ellery?" he asked, placing himself in front of the two detectives.

Campbell glanced in Liberty's direction. It was obvious that he was very pleased, not to mention hopeful, that this man would be able to finally supply them with a few answers.

"You knew her?" Campbell asked the orderly.

Luis nodded, his thick, salt-and-pepper hair not moving an inch. "Ever since she came to work in the emergency room. From the very first day, Cynthia was a really nice lady. With all her experience, she never acted as if she was above anyone. She held her temper even when some moron got in her face. Just took it all in stride," he recalled, getting a wistful, faraway look on his thin, chiseled features. "Me, I would have really told them off, but she was always cool about it." And then his face darkened with barely suppressed anger as he asked, "Do you know who did this to her?"

"That's what we're trying to find out," Liberty told the orderly. "Anything you can tell us about that dating site she was using would be really helpful."

"Just that she kept setting herself up with losers." He shook his head. "One guy more disappointing than the next."

A number of possibilities ran through Liberty's mind as she slanted a look in the orderly's direction. "And you know this for a fact?" she asked.

"I don't know about 'fact,' but I know that's what she said," the orderly told them. Then, seeing that the detectives appeared skeptical, Luis told them, "We were friends. She would tell me things she wouldn't share with the others because she was afraid she might look foolish to them."

"But she wasn't afraid she would look foolish to you?" Campbell questioned.

"No. Like I said, we were friends," Luis told the man questioning him. "Besides, she knew I wasn't about to hit on her, so she felt comfortable talking about her 'matches' with me." He looked from one detective to the other to see if they understood what he was telling them.

"Would you happen to know any of these so-called dates' names?" Campbell asked.

"I know all of them," the orderly confidently replied. He wasn't bragging, Campbell realized. The man was merely stating a simple fact.

"Could you write them down for us?" he asked.

"Sure," he told Campbell. "All I need a piece of paper and a pen."

"Coming up," Liberty said, opening her small shoulder bag and taking out the requested tools.

Taking them in hand, Luis began writing as if the fresh information would disappear if it weren't quickly preserved.

In all, there were five names. Five candidates who might or might not have been guilty of murder.

"Would you happen to know if these were aliases or their real names?" Campbell asked.

"That, I really couldn't say," he answered honestly.

At least they had something to continue investigating, Campbell thought. Folding the piece of paper, he tucked it into his pocket. "Thanks for this," he said to the orderly.

"Just find whoever did this to her," Luis told the detectives.

"We fully intend to," Liberty promised sincerely.

Leaving the hospital, Campbell looked at Liberty. "Are you hungry?"

She stared at him, startled, as they approached his vehicle. Was he saying what she thought he was saying? "You can actually eat?" she asked him.

They were dealing with homicides and multiple murders. Her own stomach felt as if was in turmoil and Liberty doubted that she could keep anything down, much less a whole meal.

"Whether I can or can't isn't the question here. I *should*," he told her with emphasis. "You've got to keep up your strength when investigating a murder—

or *murders*," he clarified, since this wasn't just about Cynthia Ellery's murder, but about thirty victims altogether... *If not more*, he couldn't help thinking.

"So in the middle of all this, we're taking a break," she said, trying to wrap her head around it.

He could tell from her tone of voice what she thought of the idea.

"No, not a 'break,' we're refueling," Campbell reworded. "Just enough to keep us going."

She sighed. She wasn't up to arguing. "Well, you're the senior investigator, so I guess I can't argue with you."

His smile seemed to bloom all over his face. "But you want to, don't you?"

"I believe this is where I'm supposed to plead the fifth," she responded.

Campbell laughed. "You're learning, Arizona," he told her. "You're learning."

He drove over to a take-out place he favored, a Chinese restaurant that had been family owned and operated for the last thirty-five years. It served Cantonese-style food, and had expanded to include Mandarin in the last couple of years.

"Do you have a certain prescribed amount I'm supposed to consume?" Liberty asked as they walked inside the restaurant.

The atmosphere was warm and welcoming.

For his part, Campbell was still getting a kick out of her as he followed the hostess to a table. "Now you're making me sound as if I'm anally retentive," he commented, waiting for the sexy looking detective from Arizona to take a seat. “Is that what you actually think?”

“I think you’re the type to make your kids eat whether they want to or not,” she told him.

“Well, luckily for them, I don’t have any,” he quipped.

“No children?” she asked.

“No, and no marriage, either,” Campbell replied.

“You could still have children,” she pointed out.

“Touché.” He laughed. “But no to either, if you’re asking. And, if you really don’t want to eat, no one is going to make you. Although I do strongly recommend it.”

She glanced at him. “You’re making it sound as if I had a choice.” Her eyes met his as she picked up the menu on the table before her. “But I don’t, do I?”

“You’re the detective,” he told her. “What do you think?”

“I think I’d better find something on the menu that I will be able to keep down,” Liberty said, opening the menu up.

His eyes smiled at her. “Good guess,” Campbell told her with approval.

Chapter 6

The server, who was the owner's grandson, brought over their orders and placed them before them. Campbell waited until the young man withdrew before he asked Liberty, "Are you sure that's all you want?"

He eyed her order: a cup of wonton soup and a couple of egg rolls. In his opinion, that wasn't enough to keep an anemic pigeon alive.

"I ordered this mostly to satisfy you," Liberty told him. "And to get me from point A to point B." She saw the skeptical look on the detective's face. "I told you, I'm not really hungry."

"Obviously," he noted. "But as I pointed out, it's not about hunger. If it was, then this could officially be thought of as a date rather than just a working late lunch."

She could feel her back going up. Why was he saying that? "Why don't we just skip the label, eat the meal and go?"

Campbell smiled at the way she summarized this entire venture. "Are you that anxious to get somewhere with this case?"

There was no point in attempting to deny how much she wanted to find answers. "And that, I'm assuming, is what makes you such a great detective," Liberty quipped.

"Oh, I'm just in it for the fascinating company," he told her.

She looked at him. Did he mean that as a slam against her? she wondered. Not that she didn't have it coming. "Well, I'm sorry you didn't luck out."

His smile went directly into her stomach, causing minor tidal waves within it. She needed to get a grip.

"I'm not complaining," he told her.

All things considered, the detective appeared to have a more than decent temperament, she decided. Taking herself in hand, Liberty shifted the focus of their conversation.

"What do you think our chances are of getting that dating site Cynthia used to open its doors to us?" she queried.

"Honestly?" Campbell asked.

When she nodded, he answered. "Small to none. We might have better luck if we go to that last restaurant Cynthia went to and look at their surveillance tapes. We might be able to see if we can get a license plate number off our victim's date's car. That way, we might be able to verify his name. Once we have that, and locate him, then we can bring him in for questioning."

This had been a slow, tedious process, but at least it was beginning to take form, she thought. For the first time in a long time, she began to feel hopeful that, eventually, she would be able to see this to its proper, well-deserved end.

Nodding, Liberty told him, "That definitely sounds good to me."

"But it's also going to take time," he pointed out, wanting her to be aware of that fact. Out of the blue, he asked, "Where are you staying?"

That was a detail she hadn't arranged yet. She had been obsessed with the big picture, not the details that made up the minutia.

"I haven't thought that far ahead," Liberty confessed. "But this looks like a big city. I figured you had to have motels here, right?"

"We do," Campbell conceded. "But even that runs into money, Arizona."

Liberty frowned at what he was saying. "I didn't exactly anticipate staying in one for free."

"I have a way around that."

She didn't follow him at first and then the radar suddenly went off in her head. She was not about to stay at his place.

"Thank you, but no thank you," Liberty told him, turning down the offer.

He looked at her in surprise, especially given the tone she'd used. "Come again?"

All right, she would put it into words that he would understand. "I'm not about to stay with you, Detective Cavanaugh."

He bit his lower lip, suppressing a laugh. "Well, tempting though that might seem—for you," he added with a grin, "I was going to suggest that you stay with one of my sisters. You have your choice between Jacqui or Blythe. If either one of them doesn't work out for you, I also have several single female cousins you could stay with."

Liberty stared at him. Granted she didn't have any relatives of her own and never had, but she doubted what he was proposing was considered standard practice amid families.

"Are you in the habit of offering up your sisters' or cousins' living quarters to perfect strangers?" she asked.

"I'd hardly call you perfect, Arizona," he said, his mouth curving. "And you're not exactly a stranger. We've been together for the better part of the day."

"Well, be that as it may, I am a stranger to them and I'm sure that they wouldn't be all that thrilled having to put me up."

"Maybe not thrilled," Campbell allowed, "but certainly happy to. We're a big, open family. It's a given."

However, Liberty still had misgivings. "Somehow, I doubt it. We'll talk about this once we meet with the company running the dating site. If we don't get anywhere with them, or the restaurant where Cynthia went on her last date, *then* we'll see what my next move is."

Campbell nodded. "I'll hold you to that," he promised with a smile. "In the meantime, can I get you anything else before we go?"

She shook her head. "No, I'm stuffed."

Compared to what she had consumed, he had had a serving of soup, lobster Cantonese and a fortune cookie, and he still felt as if he could have eaten more. But then he had always had a big appetite.

"Well, you should know," he told her. He raised his hand to get the waiter's attention, signaling that he was ready for the check.

The server, who by his familiar manner obviously knew Campbell, was quick to bring over the bill.

She waited until the man had left before asking, "How much is my share?"

Campbell took out several bills and placed them inside the folder. "Don't worry about it. It's taken care of."

Liberty drew herself up. "That's very nice of you," she said in a reserved manner, "but I like paying my own way."

"And I appreciate that," Campbell told her patiently, "but your part of the bill came to next to nothing and I really think I can handle that."

"But—"

Campbell looked at her. "Arizona, if we're going to continue working together, you are going to have to learn how to be gracious about accepting a gesture every now and then. Now, I'm paying for this meal. You can pick up the next one. Okay?"

She wasn't happy about it, but she couldn't argue

with him about everything. Like it or not, she needed him. Arguing with the man was not the right way to cement a decent working relationship.

"Okay," she responded grudgingly. Then, after a beat, added, "Thank you," as if it really pained her to utter the words.

It was hard for Campbell not to laugh, but somehow he managed to refrain.

"You're welcome, Arizona," he replied.

"By the way, that was a pretty big tip you left on the table," she commented as they left the small restaurant.

"Well, they work hard running the restaurant," he told her, "and I like the family. They've been through some pretty tough times and weathered their share of ups and downs running that place." He held open the passenger door for her. "It's my way of ensuring that my favorite restaurant sticks around a while longer."

"Why?" she asked, her curiosity aroused. "Do you think they're going to go out of business?"

"I don't think so. But I've learned to take absolutely nothing for granted these days," Campbell said.

"I know how that is." She voiced the sentiment almost to herself.

As a kid, she'd never known if the bed she went to sleep in would be the one she would be allowed to wake up in the following morning. Or if, for some reason or another, somewhere in the middle of the night she would be forced to play musical homes and be whisked off to another foster home.

"Something you'd like to share?" Campbell asked her, curious.

The sound of his voice brought Liberty back around to the present.

"No," she told him. "I would not."

He nodded, seeing the sad, almost grim expression on her face and thinking he had stumbled across some place he shouldn't be. He could feel his curiosity being aroused. That was the problem with being a detective. So many mysteries, so little time.

"Duly noted," he told her as he waited for her to buckle up.

The place that ran the Finding the Right One web site was located not too far away.

As Campbell had predicted, the people in charge of the dating site were not forthcoming with the information they needed. While they were very sympathetic about the circumstances and the reason for the request, Miles Perkins, the man in charge of managing the website, told them, "I'm afraid that my hands are tied. I can't release that information."

"You do realize that the person who availed herself of your site is now dead, right?" Liberty asked curtly.

"Yes, I realize that," Perkins told her, the soul of benevolence, "but it still doesn't allow me to release the names of the men she met on the site. I have an obligation to maintain their privacy."

Liberty was struggling very hard to hold on to her temper. "What about your obligation to Cynthia Ellery?"

The expression on the manager's face was pained as well as very sympathetic. "What happened to her is tragic," he admitted, "but it could all just be circumstantial."

Her eyes narrowed until they almost looked as if they were shooting lightning bolts. "Murder is not circumstantial, Mr. Perkins. It's a very ugly occurrence," Liberty argued.

Perkins shook his head. "I'm afraid you're going to have to talk to our lawyers," he told the two detectives. "I am very sorry."

He almost sounded sincere, but that didn't help the situation any. "Sorry is not enough to keep the next young woman from dying," Campbell informed the manager.

Perkins appeared shocked. "Wait, there have been others?"

"Thirty in all—that we know of," Campbell deliberately qualified.

"And it's one of the men she met on my dating site?" the manager questioned, vacillating between being appalled and defensive.

"That's what we're trying to ascertain," Campbell answered.

The short, personable website manager looked like a man torn between two paths, neither one of them satisfactory.

"Well," Perkins finally said, making up his mind, "until you have proof positive that one of these people was responsible, I'm afraid I can't help you."

"And we can't get our hands on 'proof positive'

until you release the information we need to trace this path to its logical conclusion," Liberty insisted.

Perkins seemed distressed but, in the end, was forced to stick to his guns. "I'm afraid I can't help you."

"Can't or won't?" Liberty asked.

The manager's eyes met hers. "Can't," Perkins repeated.

"We'll be back," Campbell promised the website manager.

Liberty did not look as if she was ready to retreat just yet. "Campbell," she protested.

But he put his arm around her shoulders and directed her toward the door. "We don't have a leg to stand on," he reminded Liberty, then told her, "We'll be back when we do."

She had no recourse but to leave with Campbell. "So we're just going to retreat?" she questioned, clearly not happy about the way this was going.

"For now, yes. I'm part of the police department. It's my job to enforce the law, Arizona, not break it whenever the mood hits me."

The expression on her face did not absolve him. "What about your job to get justice for Cynthia and all the other victims who suffered at the hands of this sick, sadistic killer?"

"Number one, getting bogged down in red tape isn't going to do Cynthia—or the others—any good. And, number two, our time can be better spent finding our way around all this."

He tried again. "Look, Arizona, I want you to get

something straight. I am on your side. I am on the victims' side. Wasting time arguing and getting nowhere with a narcissistic website manager is not going to accomplish anything. Now let's see if we can find someone at the restaurant who can be more accommodating than this jerk was. With luck, we'll get access to the surveillance tapes of the area with Cynthia's last date with 'Mr. Possible Right,'" Campbell said.

Liberty took a deep breath. She had no choice but to go along with Campbell's assessment. "Are you always this annoyingly calm and levelheaded?" she asked grudgingly.

"Always," he replied with a grin. "My dad thought it was my best feature."

She looked at him pointedly. "Well, your father was wrong."

"I'll let him know the next time I see him. Although I wouldn't hold my breath if I were you," he said, driving his vehicle to the Blue Hawaiian, which was due south.

"Oh, and why's that?" she asked, expecting to hear some sort of a flip answer from the detective.

He answered her without any fanfare. "My dad died five years ago."

His answer rendered her temporarily speechless. The casual way he just glossed over his father's death took her totally by surprise. Liberty glanced at the detective to see if he was just pulling her leg.

But one look at Campbell's profile told her he wasn't. He was serious.

"I'm very sorry for your loss," she told him. The

words always struck her as being horribly empty, but there was nothing else she could say that even began to get the message across, so she fell back on the familiar, if inadequate, saying.

"Yeah," Campbell responded. "Me, too. But if there is a heaven, then he's finally with Mom," he told Liberty, "which was the only place he ever wanted to be."

"Well, then I suppose that's comforting," she said, although Campbell wasn't all that sure she meant it.

All he could do was let her know how he felt about the situation. "Yes," Campbell answered. "It really is. It's actually the mental image I like to hang on to, Arizona." He came to a stop at a red light and glanced in Liberty's direction. "Let's see if we can find someone at the restaurant who's more helpful than the manager of that dating site."

"Amen to that," Liberty murmured.

The light turned green, and he took off.

Liberty sat back and tried to think positive thoughts, even if it wasn't in her nature.

Chapter 7

The Blue Hawaiian restaurant's parking lot was fairly packed, especially given that it wasn't a Friday or Saturday night, Liberty thought as she scanned the general area.

"Is it always like this?" she asked Campbell.

He shrugged in response. "To be truthful, I wouldn't know. But I've heard that this is a pretty popular place to take a date. Especially, if you're trying to impress her."

"You don't bring your dates here?" Liberty asked, trying to sound as if she was just making conversation and not trying to pry into his personal life. "It looks like a pretty nice place."

"I'm sure that it is, but I'm more of a spur-of-the-moment kind of guy," he confessed. "Going to a place like this takes making reservations ahead of time. In my line of work, long-term plans have a way of not working out for one reason or another." Campbell shrugged philosophically. "Maybe I'll give this place a try some day."

Because the lot turned out to be so crowded, Campbell was forced to park in one of the spaces reserved for trucks making deliveries. He made sure that he left the vehicle's flashing lights on the roof.

Liberty frowned just a little. "That should enhance the mood," she commented as they walked away from the police car and went into the restaurant.

Campbell thought of the vehicle and where it was positioned. "I just put the lights on the roof to let whoever's in charge tonight know that this vehicle is here on official police business. Otherwise, we might come out and find that it's been towed away."

That didn't strike her as likely. "Did that ever happen to you?" she asked as she walked in front of him toward the reservation desk.

"Not to me personally, but it did happen to my sister, Jacqui." The grin on his face widened as he recalled the incident. "I had no idea that she knew such colorful language."

Liberty laughed. She had never had her vehicle towed away, but she could certainly identify with that feeling of frustration the detective's sister must have experienced.

It took Liberty a moment for her eyes to adjust to the subdued lighting throughout the restaurant.

"Do they keep the lights low like this to promote

romance or to make sure that the customer doesn't see that the meal's been undercooked—or burned?" the visiting detective guessed.

"Probably a little of both," Campbell speculated. He made his way up to the desk.

An incredibly dapper and trim reservation manager glanced up and saw them approaching. It looked as if the smile he offered pained him to form. His small, brown eyes swept over them rather critically. "Do you have a reservation?" he asked coolly.

Campbell had dealt with people like this before, men impressed with what they took to be their own self-importance.

"I'm afraid not, Mr. Davis," Campbell said, reading the man's name tag as he placed his badge and police ID face-up on the desk and waited for that to register with the man.

"Oh, how can I help you, Officer… Cavanaugh, is it?" the manager asked, raising his eyes to the detective's face.

"That's *Detective* Cavanaugh," Campbell corrected with no emotion. "And you can direct us to where you keep your surveillance tapes. But first, were you here three days ago after 6:00 p.m.?" he asked the pompous little man.

It seemed to Liberty that Davis appeared to withdraw into himself, as if bracing, even though he didn't appear to know for what.

"I was," Davis finally replied crisply. His eyes darted back and forth between the duo at his desk. He was obviously waiting for more.

Campbell held up Cynthia's picture for him. "Does this woman look familiar to you?" he asked.

The manager squinted as he looked at image. "Possibly," he answered vaguely. "I see a lot of people here. The Hawaiian is a very popular restaurant," he proudly informed the couple before him. And then his rather high forehead suddenly wrinkled. "Why are you looking for her? Did she do something?"

"Yes," Liberty answered, losing her patience with Davis, whom she felt was playing games with them. "She died."

Her statement horrified the overly fastidious little man at the reservation desk. His small dark eyes seemed to grow to almost twice their size.

"How?" Even as he asked, the answer seemed to hit him. "Oh, wait, is she that woman they had on the news?"

Unaware of what Davis might have been exposed to, Campbell answered, "Most likely."

Davis looked as if his mouth had suddenly gone completely dry.

"And you think the killer brought her here before he—?" Davis couldn't get himself to finish the question. The mere suggestion of what he was thinking seemed to stick in his throat.

"We don't know," Campbell answered. "That's why we'd like to view your surveillance tapes from that night. I'm assuming that you have several cameras going at all times, monitoring your restaurant both inside and out."

The reservation manager's face paled by several

shades. For just a moment, he looked as if his knees would buckle.

Mopping his brow, he said, "Yes, yes, we do. You actually thought this monster brought her here first before he…?" Davis stopped, unable to complete the question.

"Like Detective Cavanaugh said, we don't know what to think yet," Liberty told the reservation manager. "We're investigating all the possibilities. That's why we'd like to be able to see your surveillance tapes."

The manager looked at Liberty as if he hadn't even realized that she was asking him a question until just this very moment.

He shook his head as if to clear it. "I'm sorry," he said, realizing that she wasn't there with the detective as his companion but in some official capacity. "And you are?"

Getting really annoyed with you, fella, Liberty thought.

As if reading her mind, Campbell stepped in, ready to divert any possible problem before it could form. "This is Detective Lawrence," he said by way of an introduction. "She's a consultant from Arizona here to help us out with this case. There have been several women killed there by this man."

Davis turned even paler than he already had. It didn't take much for him to put two and two together. "You mean we're dealing with a…a serial killer?" The man was clearly traumatized.

"That appears to be the case," Campbell replied.

"But we really don't know that for a fact yet. We can tell you more once we view the tapes," he repeated, pinning Davis with a probing look. He wanted to move this along as quickly as he could. "So, if you would take us to where you house your surveillance monitors, we'll be out of your way."

"But I can't leave you with them," Davis protested. By the expression on his face, doing so would clearly be a violation of protocol, as far as he was concerned.

"Then stay in the room with us. Do whatever you have to do as long as we get to review the tapes," Campbell said, trying to curb his impatience.

In the end, the reservation manager called over one of his assistants. He had the young woman take the two detectives over to where the security tape equipment was housed.

The assistant, Polly Howard, appeared to be new at her job—but exceptionally eager to help. "Are you two *really* detectives with the police department?" she asked.

"Yes, we're really with the police department," Campbell replied.

"Mr. Davis looks really spooked," she confided, lowering her voice. "Did he do something? I mean, other than point out how everyone who works for him is just always falling short of his standards?" Polly asked in an even lower voice.

Campbell had no intentions of being sucked into any sort of a discussion regarding the reservation manager. "How about you show us where those surveillance tapes are? And then we can take it from there."

Instead of becoming embarrassed and backing away from the subject, the young woman happily continued talking and speculating.

Polly led them into a small room. There appeared to be only one working monitor set up within the room to enable viewing the surveillance tapes.

Pointing to the monitor, Polly hovered on the sidelines. She didn't look as if she wanted to leave.

"Is there anything else I can do?" she asked.

The restaurant grew noisier and the increased noise was beginning to invade their space.

"You can shut the door on your way out," Liberty told her in all seriousness.

The assistant looked to Campbell for instructions, turning her doe-like eyes in his direction. "Is that what you want, Detective?" she asked Campbell almost breathlessly.

"Yes," he confirmed. "We can take it from here," Campbell assured her.

Disappointed, even Polly's hair appeared to fall slightly. "I'll be right outside if you need me," she said.

"Good to know," he acknowledged.

Davis's assistant was already forgotten by the time Campbell started to insert the tape labeled two days ago.

Liberty looked at him. "You know how to work these things?" she asked, eyeing Campbell skeptically.

He gestured at the surveillance monitor. "How hard can it be?"

"So, no," Liberty concluded. Moving closer to the space where Campbell was standing, she put out her hand and said, "Give it to me."

It was his turn to doubt her. "*You* know how to work this equipment?" he asked, waiting for her to reply to his question.

She took exception to his tone. "I'm from Calhoun, not Sleepy Hollow. You'd be surprised at the kind of technology we have in that little town," she assured him. "Now let me work."

Campbell inclined his head and then saluted. "Yes, ma'am."

"And hold the sarcasm," she said.

He grinned at her. "Consider it held."

Liberty decided she would be better off if she simply ignored the tall, handsome detective and just focused on the video tapes.

Since there was only one monitor for viewing, it proved to be rather slow going. They wound up spelling each other to make sure they wouldn't miss anything and also to keep their eyes from crossing, thanks to too much close viewing.

But finally they were finished.

"I think I might just wind up giving up watching TV for a while," Liberty told Campbell, shutting her eyes and rubbing the bridge of her nose. "The worst part of it is, after all that, we only got a partial license plate number *and* it looks like her date wound up leaving the restaurant without her." She frowned. "What that means is anyone's guess."

"That doesn't mean that they didn't get together later on the next day," he pointed out.

"The day she died," Liberty emphasized.

Campbell's eyes meet hers. "Exactly."

Liberty dragged her hand through her hair. "So how do we find him? We only have that partial license plate and a less than stellar video of his face."

Campbell thought over what she had just said. "That might be enough."

She didn't see how, but she was willing to be convinced. "Keep talking," Liberty said, eager to grab at anything.

"I have this cousin who works in the CSI lab," Campbell told her. "She works miracles with and without the computer."

"Miracles, huh?" Liberty asked. "What kind of miracles?"

He merely smiled at the visiting detective. "You'll see. First thing we need to do is make a copy of this tape. And then I'll take this to Valri tomorrow."

"Tomorrow?" Liberty repeated, clearly disappointed. She was shifting from foot to foot. "Why not today?"

He was surprised that she had to ask. "Because it is almost tomorrow and, as good as Valri is, sometimes she needs to get at least a few minutes of sleep before she's ready to go again. Now let's see if we can find that assistant so we can tell her that we're through here for now, but that we're going to need a copy of this portion of the tape."

"If it's that late, maybe Polly already went home?" Liberty told him.

As it turned out, Polly hadn't gone anywhere. The moment Campbell opened the door, the faithful little assistant came all but bounding into the room.

"Can I help you?" she asked eagerly, her question directed to Campbell.

"Yes," Campbell said, taking the surveillance tape from Liberty and handing it to the young woman. "We need a copy of this tape."

"Just one copy?" Polly asked. She almost sounded disappointed.

"Just the one," Campbell confirmed. "We'd really appreciate it," he added for good measure.

"Is the killer on this?" the assistant asked, her voice dropping even lower, as if the killer might overhear her.

"That's where the investigating part comes in," Campbell told her with a wink.

Polly's eyes were all but shining with anticipation. "Sure, sure, I get it. But if you find out, will you tell me?"

"If we find out, *you'll* find out," Liberty assured the young woman.

The assistant all but skipped out of the room to make the requested copy.

"Why did you tell her that?" Campbell asked. They both knew they couldn't release that kind of information to the public.

"To get her moving," Liberty told him. "She looked as if she thought she was suddenly part of a murder mystery. There's no harm in fueling her imagination. Who knows, maybe in a strange way, it'll keep her safe."

"The killer preys on nurses, remember?" That meant that this little assistant was safe, Campbell thought.

"I know, but there might be some other killer out there who doesn't make that distinction," Liberty pointed out. "Doesn't hurt to keep a young innocent like that on her toes," she told Campbell.

"You're right," he agreed. "It doesn't."

The assistant returned within ten minutes. She was holding up a fresh copy of the surveillance tape she had just made.

"Here you go," Polly announced. "That tape you requested." She handed it to Campbell. "Now, you'll remember to keep your promise, won't you?"

Liberty could see that he was drawing a blank. "About telling her the minute we find out if the man on the tape is our killer," she said, refreshing Campbell's memory. "Of course Detective Cavanaugh will let you know. If it wasn't for you, he wouldn't have a tape to help him make that comparison, would you, Detective Cavanaugh?"

"I definitely wouldn't," he said, already on his way to the door. "Thanks for all your help and take care of yourself."

Polly sent them—mainly Campbell—on their way with a dreamy sigh.

Chapter 8

Liberty knew what Campbell was up to and she was not about to allow him to do it.

"It's after eleven, Cavanaugh," she pointed out as they drove away from the restaurant.

"Well, I guess that answers my question if you can tell time or not, Arizona," hc quipped.

She gave him an icy stare. "Very funny. You know what I'm getting at."

"Probably," Campbell replied. "But just for fun, enlighten me."

Shc found herself fighting the urge to strangle the man. "I am not about to allow you to wake up one of your sisters—or one of your cousins—so that I can have a place to crash. Just take me back to the police station so I can get my car and then point me toward the nearest hotel or motel. I'll take care of the rest from there."

He just shook his head. "Sorry, but I can't have you wandering around Aurora at this time of night."

"But I'm a police detective," she noted, flabbergasted at the objection he had just raised.

Campbell added an addendum. "Yes, but in a strange city."

She was just too tired to argue coherently with him. "All right, you must have beds in the squad room where your detectives can crash when they're working through the night." She sighed, leaning back against her seat. "Take me there."

"I have an alternative," Campbell said.

Alerted, she shot him another annoyed look. "I'm not sure I want to hear it."

He ignored her protest. "I'll take you back to my place," Campbell offered. "I've got a spare bedroom. You can crash there."

"No," she said flatly, wondering what it took to get through to this pigheaded, stubborn man.

"You have nothing to worry about," he assured her. "I'll even take a pledge of celibacy if that makes you feel better."

She doubted if the man knew the meaning of the word *celibacy*. He just didn't look like the type. However, she was willing to be entertained.

"That would almost be worth it," Liberty said with a laugh.

Almost, she thought, *but not quite.*

Campbell glanced in her direction. "Why?" he asked. "Would you try to entice me?"

The grin he flashed her managed to get under her skin.

"I make it a point never to play with fire," she informed him coolly.

"You're telling me that you're not even a little bit intrigued?" Campbell asked. His eyes were back on the road, but she could have sworn she felt them studying her.

"Not so much as an iota," she replied.

If this were another time and another place, maybe she might have been a little intrigued, she conceded silently. But right now she was focused on doing whatever it took to solve this case and absolutely *nothing* else mattered.

"Okay," he told her. "This is what's going to happen. I will bring you to the police station so you can collect your car. But then, in the interest of getting an early start, I'd appreciate it if you just follow me to my place." Before she could protest, he quickly added, "I promise you'll be safer than if you were staying in a convent." To add weight to his statement, he even crossed his heart.

Did he really think she was that naive? "I'm not sure about that."

"Oh?"

"I looked you up on social media," she told the detective. "According to that, you have quite a reputation."

"Not that I'm not flattered that you took the time

to do that," Campbell told her, "but you're also bright enough to know that things are greatly exaggerated on social media."

"Maybe," she allowed, "but I live by the saying that I would rather be safe than sorry. And right now, the most important thing in the world to me—the *only* thing—is finding this serial killer and getting him off the street."

Campbell could definitely understand that. Yet he could also sense that there was more to it than that. "And if we find him, will you tell me why you are so obsessed with getting *this* man?"

She stared at his profile, astonished. "Why would you even ask that? Catching the bad guy and making him pay for all those killings he committed doesn't seem like enough to you?"

"Oh, it definitely would be," he answered. "Nevertheless, I get the sense there's something more going on here, and I'm the type who can't sleep well until I have all the answers."

She laughed dryly in response to his words. "Something tells me, Detective Cavanaugh, that you don't sleep much."

He shrugged just as he pulled into the station parking area. "I get enough."

There were a minimum number of vehicles parked in the lot. Campbell pulled his car up beside hers, then engaged the hand brake and turned off the engine.

"So, what'll it be?" he asked, turning to face Liberty. "Did I manage to talk you into following me to my apartment?" Even in the sparse lighting, he could see the reluctant look on the visiting detective's face. "There is one more alternative."

"Another alternative," she repeated, amused despite herself. "Okay, I'm listening."

"I could take you over to my uncle Andrew and his wife Rose's house. They're the unofficial patriarchs of the family. You'd have no reason to complain about being put up at their house."

"It's late. They're probably asleep. I'm not about to wake up older people," she said, enumerating just some of her reasons.

Campbell laughed. "I won't tell them you said that. Look, they're patriarchs of what amounts to a police dynasty. That means that they wake up for emergencies. It's a given. And calling them 'older' will *not* endear you to them no matter how understanding they are."

"I am still not going to be responsible for disturbing them," she informed him in a tone that said she was not about to change her mind.

Campbell shook his head as he blew out a breath. "You really are a hard person to negotiate with, Arizona."

"I wasn't aware that we were 'negotiating,'" she retorted.

"*That* might be part of the problem," Campbell told her. "All right," he said, his negotiations, not to mention his patience, reaching their final stretch. "What's it going to be? I've given you a choice of picking one of my sisters, one of my cousins, or the family patriarch—or me."

"You forgot about going to a hotel," Liberty reminded him.

"No, I didn't forget. That was never a viable option as far as I was concerned. Now pick," he urged.

Liberty frowned. "You realize that this whole thing is rigged, right?"

He looked at her innocently. "I have no idea what you're talking about, Arizona."

"Uh-huh," she answered, rolling her eyes. This was getting her nowhere and she had a feeling the detective wasn't about to give up until she agreed to one of his options. Tired of going around in circles, she said, "All right, we'll go to your place."

"Glad to hear that you've come around," Campbell told her.

Come around, my foot, she thought. But she was in no mood to continue the back-and-forth on the subject. Frowning at him, she said, "You should be aware of the fact that I sleep with my gun."

He gave no indication of being surprised or caught off guard. "Duly noted. I hope the two of you are very happy together. Now are you ready to go?"

She supposed she had no choice. And, at bottom, she did believe that she would be safe. Ultimately, she believed that the detective wouldn't try anything. She'd take him at his word that he was honestly just taking her to his apartment so that she could get some rest.

But if for some reason she had miscalculated, Cavanaugh would be the one to pay the price, she assured herself.

"All right," Liberty said out loud as she got out of his vehicle and got into hers. "Lead the way to your place."

He was sorely tempted to say something snappy, but refrained. Instead he merely said, "It's close by. You won't regret this."

"I already do," she answered. She waved at his car. "Lead the way to your apartment before I decide to go to sleep right here."

"Can't have that," Campbell told her. "My place is three miles from here. Can you make it?" he asked, thinking how tired she'd just said she was feeling.

Her smile was slightly lopsided. "Can I make it? In my sleep."

"That's what I'm afraid of," he joked. "I'm still going to go slow."

"Why?" she asked suspiciously. Wasn't the whole point to get there quickly?

"So I can keep an eye on you in my rearview mirror," he told her.

Liberty's mind did a double-take. "I don't know whether to be touched by this display of thoughtfulness on your part, or insulted because you think I'm incapable of going from point A to point B."

"Go with touched," he counseled with a grin. "It's simpler that way. Now, if there's nothing else, let's get a move on."

"Well, now that you've mentioned it…" Liberty began, ready to rethink the whole idea of crashing at his apartment.

"Good, let's go," he declared, pretending he hadn't

heard her attempt to extend the argument. Starting his car, he glanced up into his rearview mirror.

Campbell mentally crossed his fingers as he pulled out of his spot. He released a sigh of relief when he saw her start up her own vehicle.

Liberty followed him from the parking lot and into the street.

So far, so good, he thought.

Even so, Campbell kept checking for Liberty's car in his rearview mirror the entire short distance from the police station to his garden apartment: Sunflower Creek Apartments.

He pulled into his carport and got out in time to indicate to Liberty that she should find a spot in guest parking. Because of the hour, there were only a few spots left.

Campbell walked over to the area and waited until she parked her car.

"I'm flattered," she said as she exited her vehicle and popped open her trunk. She took out the overnight bag she had packed. He started to take it from her but Liberty held on to the straps. "I can carry it," she informed him. "You're already going the whole nine yards, escorting me to your apartment and to a spot in guest parking. Or do you want to carry my bag because you're thinking I'm going to bolt at the last minute?"

"I wasn't thinking about you bolting. But it is dark," he pointed out. "You might not find your way to the right apartment. I've seen residents go stumbling around at night, looking for their own door.

Of course, they'd had a few too many at the time," he added with what Liberty could only view as a wicked grin.

"When would I have had the time to imbibe?" she couldn't help asking.

"Good point," he agreed. "But it is dark and you don't know your way. Why don't you just say 'thanks' and let it go at that?"

By now they had reached the bottom of the stairway that led up to his second-floor apartment. Gritting her teeth, Liberty forced out the words. "Thank you."

His hand on the railing, Campbell pretended to grasp it to steady himself while putting his other hand to his chest. "I'm overwhelmed," he declared.

She turned to look at him and issue one final warning.

"If you're on the level, thank you. But if you have any ideas..." Her voice trailed off, leaving the warning unspoken.

"I'm a police detective. I *always* have ideas," Campbell told her. "But I promise not any of them pertain to you."

Which, at this point, Campbell thought, *is a lie*. Since she'd walked into his squad room, several ideas had sprung up in his mind and formed around her.

But he was smart enough to know that breathing even one word of that to this extremely sexy Arizona detective would spell the end of their working relationship, not to mention any other potential relationship that even had a prayer of happening anywhere in the near or even foreseeable future.

His two-bedroom apartment was not only located on the second floor, it also overlooked a rather large communal pool.

All in all, the first word that came to Liberty's mind was *peaceful*.

When he unlocked his apartment door for her, it was also, considering the fact that a bachelor lived there, incredibly neat, Liberty thought.

"Was the maid just here?" she asked, looking around at the immediate area before she set down the small, overnight bag she had brought in.

Campbell looked at her curiously. "What maid?" he asked.

"Yours, I'm assuming," she answered.

He still wasn't clear on what she was referring to. "Why would you think I have a maid?"

"Well, because—" Liberty gestured around the living room. When he still didn't say anything, she filled in the blanks for him. "It's so neat. You either have a maid or you—" It suddenly hit her. "Your girlfriend did this." He hadn't said anything about having a live-in girlfriend, but what other explanation could there be? There weren't even any dishes in the sink.

"Nope, no girlfriend," he said. "I would have mentioned one before inviting you over," Campbell assured her.

She was at a loss as she looked around again. "Then how—"

"There is another explanation," Campbell told her.

"And that is?" she asked, curious.

"I was raised by a mother who insisted that we all carry our own weight. We took turns doing the chores, which included, among other things, cleaning up after ourselves as well as anyone else in the family who needed overseeing at the time. To answer your question once and for all, I am not involved with anyone at the moment, so there won't be anyone turning up either in the apartment or on my doorstep at any point. Now, if you're ready to move on to something more immediate, let me show you to your room so that you can sack out and get some rest—unless there's something else?" he asked, looking at her.

Liberty had to admit that he had answered everything, and she was out of things to ask. "No, you've answered everything sufficiently."

"Good. Your room is this way." Before she could reach for it, he picked up her overnight bag. "And I have no intention of wrestling you for this overnight case," he informed her as he walked toward the back of the apartment without looking in her direction. "So just deal with it."

For once, she didn't offer a protest.

Campbell smiled to himself as he led the way to the spare bedroom.

One battle down, a thousand to go.

Chapter 9

Liberty had to admit that she was more than a little impressed. The double bed in the spare bedroom not only had clean sheets, but when she pulled back the covers, they looked to be crisp as well.

"There are fresh towels in there," Campbell pointed out, indicating the small adjacent bathroom. "You have your own bathroom so you don't have to worry about sharing one. And if you need anything else," he went on," just let me know. I'm right down the hall." He nodded toward his own bedroom. "Otherwise, I'll see you in the morning, Arizona."

And with that, since she hadn't said anything, he was gone.

Despite the fact that Campbell had brought in her overnight case and left it on the floor beside the bed, she decided to sleep in her clothes—just in case. It was a habit she'd developed during all those "first nights" she had spent in so many different bedrooms. A habit born out of the fact that if anything went wrong—the way it had in one of the foster homes she had gone to—she was ready to run if she had to.

Because of that incident—her foster parents' teenaged son who'd felt anyone in his house was there for his own personal pleasure—it always took her a while to trust someone.

By the time Florence had taken her in and become her foster mother, trusting someone had been a luxury Liberty felt she couldn't afford. Consequently, it had taken her a long time to be won over. But Florence had never given up. The nurse had kept at her until her walls finally came down.

Stretching out on the bed, Liberty sighed. The bed turned out to be exceedingly comfortable, but she still couldn't relax.

You would think that after all the different beds she had slept in, falling asleep wouldn't be a problem. She should have the ability to fall asleep at the drop of a hat, especially in one that was this comfortable.

But she couldn't.

Liberty was just too tense. And the good-looking detective had next to nothing to do with it. A very large part of her was afraid that this investigation was going to turn out to be just another wild-goose chase that would lead her nowhere.

"Knock it off, Lib," she lectured herself. "What did Florence always say? Negative thoughts lead to negative energy and that'll get you absolutely nowhere. You're going to find the dirtbag who killed all those women even if it takes you forever."

Clinging to that thought as if it were the proverbial life preserver, Liberty finally managed to fall asleep.

When Liberty ventured out of the guest bedroom nearly seven hours later, she found that Campbell was already up and in the kitchen, puttering around by the stove.

Cooking.

Something else she didn't think was typical of the male of the species. At least, not any male she was acquainted with.

The scent of rich, freshly brewed coffee caught her attention and drew her in.

Campbell looked up and over his shoulder just as she entered the kitchen. Walking away from the stove, he smiled a greeting at her. "Hi, did you sleep well?"

She didn't want to admit that she'd had trouble sleeping in a new bed, so she merely shrugged and said, "I slept."

"But not well," Campbell guessed, reading between the lines.

She supposed it wasn't that unusual a trait, so she admitted, "It always takes me time to adjust to a new bed."

Campbell took the information in stride. "I guess I'm lucky that way. I can fall asleep hanging from a hook in the closet."

Liberty laughed at the image that created in her head. "I'd like to see that sometime."

The homicide detective smiled at her. "I'll keep that in mind. Would you like some breakfast?" He indicated the frying pan on the stove.

She stared at Campbell. The question came automatically, even if she could see what was happening for herself. "You cook?"

"I cook." He would have thought that would have been self-evident because of his question. "Is that a yes then?"

"I like living dangerously," Liberty wisecracked. "So, yes."

He offered her a choice. "Scrambled? Poached? Sunny-side up?"

"Whatever is easiest," Liberty answered, then felt obligated to add, "And, for the record, I'm very impressed."

His eyes met hers. "Well then, let's hope I keep impressing you."

Liberty had no answer why those simple words would send such a warm shiver shimmying up and down her spine, but they did.

Big-time.

"Well, to make that happen," she told him, "all you have to do is help me track down this SOB."

Campbell grinned as he turned to the stove to finish making breakfast. "Don't ask for much, do you?"

"I didn't say it would be easy," she reminded the detective.

"No," he agreed as he placed a plate of scrambled

eggs, toast and bacon right in front of her. "You did not. But it's a challenge I'd be more than happy to try to meet," he told her.

And, for once, she felt he was being serious. She had no reason to doubt him.

"Valri, I've been singing your praises to this visiting detective from Calhoun, Arizona," Campbell announced to his cousin as they walked into the computer lab a little more than an hour later.

Valri Cavanaugh Brody looked up from her computer. But rather than make eye contact with her cousin or the woman who had walked in with him, the much-touted wizard of the computer lab turned her eyes up to the ceiling.

"I don't remember hearing any predictions about snow today," she said.

Liberty looked quizzically at Campbell. Before he could say anything, Valri went on to say, "So why am I on the receiving end of such a snow job?"

"No snow job," Campbell denied. "Everyone knows you are a wizard when it comes to finding answers on the computer even if looks as if there just aren't any to be found."

Valri eyed him with a knowing expression. "Very flattering, Cam, but you still have to go to the end of the line. There are just so many hours in the day and just so much of me to go around."

"That's a shame," Campbell told her placatingly. He then went on to make the introductions as if Valri hadn't said anything. "Arizona, meet my cousin, Valri Cavanaugh Brody. Valri, this is—"

"Detective Liberty Lawrence," Liberty said, taking half a step forward and putting her hand out to the blonde sitting at the very impressive computer monitor. She wasn't about to have the woman thinking that her name was Arizona.

"She—now *we*," Campbell told his cousin, "are on the trail of a serial killer. His victims total thirty women, possibly more. Show her the list, Arizona."

Liberty obliged, taking the folded sheet out of the messenger bag hanging from her shoulder.

Valri took the paper and looked at it. "You're sure this is all because of one person?" she asked.

Liberty nodded. "Oh, I'm sure," she answered. "This is all over the course of four years." And then she went into some particulars. "He has a very unique signature. He only preys on nurses between the ages of twenty-five and fifty. He strangles them using piano wire."

Valri took in the information. "That does sound unique. Anything else?"

Liberty nodded. "Until recently, he had confined his 'spree' to Arizona, except for a couple of killings he did in between in Nevada and one in New Mexico. But now he's spread his 'net' to include Southern California. The last victim we have was trying to meet men via a dating service. Thanks to information from one of her friends, we have a partial license plate number and a partial image of the last man she met through the site.

"It just might be a coincidence, but right now, that guy's our only lead," Liberty told Valri.

"We're planning on interviewing the family members of the last few victims, who were from California," Campbell added, "but we thought that anything you could add to our very sparse collection of information would be gratefully appreciated."

Valri glanced at her cousin. "I take it you're assuming that you're no longer at the end of the line?"

He couldn't read her expression, so Campbell made his plea. "Valri, the guy's a serial killer and it's only a matter of time before he's going to get itchy and kill again. If the past is any indication, it will be soon."

Valri sighed and looked toward the door leading into the office. "I knew I should have asked Uncle Brian to put a lock on my door. A lock," she added, looking at Campbell and feeling as if this argument had already been lost, "that you wouldn't be able to pick."

He knew better than to celebrate a victory. "Why, Valri, you wound me."

"Don't tempt me," his cousin warned, already trying to figure out how to squeeze this in with the rest of her mountain of work.

Rather than Campbell saying something flip in response, it was Liberty who spoke up.

"Thank you," she said to Valri. "I know this isn't your usual protocol, but it does mean a great deal to me."

Valri looked at the other woman, picking up something in her tone. "You make it sound personal."

Liberty was about to shrug off Valri's assumption but then wrestled with her better judgment. Maybe if she told her, Valri wouldn't be so undecided about finding the time to help.

"It is," Liberty admitted quietly. "He killed my foster mother."

Both Valri and Campbell were momentarily stunned.

Valri recovered first. "I am very sorry for your loss, Liberty. I realize that those words don't even begin to cover it, but at least it does give me a reason to bump the case up to the head of the line—at least for a little while," she qualified.

The wattage of the smile Campbell flashed at his cousin was nearly blinding.

"Thanks, Val. You're the best," he declared. "And you really should have an assistant helping you."

"I do," she told him. That was the odd thing about this. The more assistants she had, the bigger the workload became. "I have three of them," she told Campbell. "However, that doesn't begin to put a dent in the workload." She looked over at her desk and shook her head. The piles were overflowing.

"You know, for one of the safest cities in the country, you wouldn't think there would be this many caseloads, but there are… Okay, go," Valri ordered, waving them away. "I have work to do—and so do you. Keep me abreast of anything you find out," she instructed her cousin.

"Count on it," Campbell promised.

He headed for the door. Opening it, he waited for Liberty. The latter walked through the doorway without looking in his direction.

They walked in silence to the elevator. When it arrived, they got into the empty car and Campbell pressed for the first floor. When the doors closed, he finally broke the silence.

"So that's why."

Liberty looked at him as if she had forgotten he was with her. "Excuse me?"

"I said so that's why this case is so important to you," Campbell said, extrapolating on his initial reaction.

She shouldn't have said anything, Liberty upbraided herself. But she had really wanted Valri to look into the case for them—now and not when it came up in the queue. The more help she got with this, Liberty thought, the better.

"Every case is important," she informed Campbell coolly.

He wasn't about to argue with that, but he knew what she was trying to do. She was trying to cover up the truth. "Don't give me platitudes, Arizona. Now, are you referring to that woman you mentioned earlier? Florence?" he specified.

"That doesn't matter," Liberty told him, attempting to try to shrug it off.

"Yes, it does," he told her firmly. "It matters to you and it matters to this case. Now, are you going to tell me if I'm right, or am I going to have to look up every one of those women in the list and pull up all the details from the various news stories until I find out if Florence was the person responsible for you taking up this quest?"

The elevator door opened and they both got out. Liberty looked at the detective. She could tell that Campbell wasn't about to let up until she gave him the answer he was looking for.

Resigned, Liberty said, "I'd rather not go into it on the first floor of the police station."

"Fair enough." As long as she answered his question, he wasn't choosey about where she did it. "Pick the place."

She thought for a second. "You have a local diner around here?"

"No, but we have coffee shops," he told her. "I'll take you to the closest one."

She nodded. Going to a coffee shop would buy her some time to collect herself, Liberty thought. She didn't want to just blurt out details at random. Florence had been a private person and she knew the woman wouldn't appreciate having her life dissected by strangers, although she also knew that if this case had a prayer of getting solved, anonymity was going to have to be surrendered, at least in part.

Liberty discovered that she didn't have as much time as she thought. The coffee shop Campbell took her to turned out to be located a block and a half away from the police station.

The coffee shop wasn't crowded, but it wasn't exactly empty, either. But then, given its location, it never really was.

"What'll you have?" Campbell asked Liberty as he parked in the lot in front of the shop.

"Doesn't matter," she answered. "Just something to hold on to when I talk."

He thought that was an odd way to put it. "This isn't an interrogation," he told her. "Just one partner filling in another."

"We're partners now?" she questioned. Did he think she was stupid? She wasn't about to be put at ease so quickly.

Or fooled, either.

"Yeah, we're partners," Campbell answered.

"And when did this happen?" she asked. "I was just the 'visiting detective from Arizona' a little while ago."

"Sometime during our visit to Valri." When she'd had told his cousin why the case was so important to her, Campbell had found himself feeling her pain. "The point is we're partners and we'll continue to be partners until we either put this to bed, or you get sick of being out here and take off for your home ground."

Liberty looked at him. "Got an answer for everything, don't you?" she asked.

Campbell detected a bit of admiration beneath the sarcasm in her voice.

"I give it my best shot," he told her. "And I've got an entire family in law enforcement to draw on, so that makes me more or less prepared for anything. What'll you have, Arizona?" he asked, nodding toward the coffee counter.

"Coffee."

"There're a lot of different kinds to choose from," he said, waving his hand at the menu board.

"Just coffee," Liberty repeated.

"Okay, coffee it is," Campbell obliged. Turning to the person behind the counter, he ordered, "Two coffees, please."

The squeaky-clean server smiled obligingly. "Very good, sir. And the name, please?" he asked, taking out a magic marker.

"Cavanaugh," Campbell answered.

The server sighed. "Yeah, like that's unique," he murmured under his breath, writing the last name on each of the two containers.

"I take it your whole family comes here?" Liberty asked.

"Other than Murphy's, this is their favorite watering hole," Campbell said, stepping to the side to wait for the coffees.

"Murphy's?" she asked, unfamiliar with the name. "What's that?"

"It's a cop bar owned and run by a retired cop. We can go there sometime," he offered.

At this point, she wasn't ready to commit to anything, "We'll see," she answered vaguely and then added, "If we wind up having something to celebrate."

Chapter 10

Instead of taking the two containers from the clerk behind the counter and going outside, Campbell brought the containers over to a small table for two on the side of the coffee shop. Indicating that Liberty take a seat, he did the same.

After a moment, Liberty lowered herself into the chair.

"Take your time," Campbell counseled. "Talk whenever you feel you're up to it." Mentally, he was prepared to wait her out.

Liberty frowned slightly, staring into the coffee container. The overhead light shimmered on the dark surface.

Ever so slowly, she began to open up.

"Her name was Florence," she told him, then added simply, "And she's the reason I'm not in prison."

Whatever Campbell was expecting to hear, it certainly wasn't that. He wanted to say something but wasn't about to interrupt her, or she might stop talking again.

"That was the general consensus of what my future held," Liberty said, "given the path I was on. But Florence kept insisting I was better than that. She told me that she had faith in me." A fond expression played on her face. "I fought her all the way. But, ultimately, because of her, I graduated high school then went on to college. After that, I went on to the police academy.

"Florence never got married or had any kids, so I guess I was her whole family and she was mine," Liberty said, talking to a spot on the wall right above Campbell's head. It seemed easier that way for her. She let out a long breath. "Florence was a force to be reckoned with and so full of life, I just couldn't believe she would ever die. Until she did," she added quietly.

"What happened?" Campbell coaxed when she stopped talking.

The memory rose in her mind's eye like a terrible specter. "I was working at the Calhoun police station at the time, when my sergeant took me aside and said they had found Florence's body behind a dumpster in an alley. She was still in her nurse's uniform." Liberty's voice broke.

His heart went out to her. Campbell put a comforting hand over hers. She was clearly suffering. "You don't have to say any more."

But now that she had started, Liberty was determined to face her demons and get this all out. "She had been strangled with a piano wire. It didn't make any sense to me at the time. There didn't seem to be a connection because she neither taught nor played piano. And I know she wasn't putting herself out on any dating sites."

"Maybe she was just looking for companionship," Campbell suggested.

Liberty shook her head. "She was a big believer in 'if it was meant to be, it would happen.' The only conclusion I could come to was that her killer had to either be a patient at the hospital, or maybe a former patient."

"I take it you stayed close," Campbell surmised.

"Yes," she answered emphatically.

"Did she ever mention anyone she had a problem with, or that she was afraid of?" Campbell asked her.

Liberty shook her head. He wasn't asking her anything she hadn't asked herself a hundred times before. "The only thing I can think of is displacement."

"Displacement?" Campbell questioned, not sure what she meant.

Liberty nodded. "The way I see it is that the killer is obviously trying to kill someone from his past. You had to know Florence. She was like a stern mother figure. Always trying to help, but always keeping a steady hand over things." Her smile faded as she released a shaky breath. "At the time, I was too broken up to think straight—and I had no idea that the guy was a serial killer. I thought Florence being killed was an isolated incident that just didn't make any sense to me."

"But now we have more pieces to work with," Campbell reminded her. "Or we will once we start interviewing victims' families."

In an odd way, Liberty found comfort in his words, as well as in finally being able to talk about Florence.

She looked at the man sitting opposite her, waiting for him to say something that would make her regret sharing this with him. But he didn't.

Instead, Campbell told her, "We'll find this guy, Arizona. It might take a while, but sooner or later, he'd going to slip up and then he'll wind up paying for all the lives he ended so prematurely."

She was surprised that the detective was making this promise to her. "Isn't it supposed to be against your training to make promises like that? You know, ones you have no way of knowing if you can keep?"

He didn't look fazed about being taken to task. "Maybe that's what it says in some official handbook," Campbell admitted, "but in my family, the only reason *any* of us go into law enforcement is so that we can protect and serve—and we honestly believe that. The day we stop feeling that way is the day we hand in our shields and go into something else." He looked at her coffee container. She had managed to drain it without realizing it. "Ready to go?" he asked, nodding at the empty container.

Liberty wasn't aware that she'd had any of her coffee, much less finished it. With a smile, she crumpled the container, ready to throw it out. "I guess I am," she replied.

As they rose from the table, he let her lead the way out. He had one more question to ask her.

"How are you coping with your loss now?" Campbell asked.

She was surprised that he would ask, and touched as well. "I'll let you know once we catch this bastard," she told him.

He completely understood.

They went back to Campbell's squad room at the police station. Commandeering a bulletin board and placing it in a conference room, he tacked up each and every one of the victims' names and left a space just beneath the names for any pertinent details they'd gather during the investigation. The slightest thing just might wind up affecting the individual case.

Peering at the board gave Liberty a hollow feeling. "That looks pretty daunting," she commented, staring at the empty spaces.

"It's just a board that hasn't been filled up yet," Campbell assured her. "It's only a matter of time until it takes shape."

She looked at him, beginning to feel that she had never met anyone quite like Campbell. "Is everyone in your family this optimistic?" she wanted to know.

"It's a prerequisite for being in the family," he deadpanned. "It's also in our DNA," he confided. "Okay, let's get Choi in here and we'll each take ten names to look up. Once we put the background information together, we'll question however many family members we find. Or in absence of that, any of the victims' friends we can find."

"Are you sure this is all okay with your boss?" Liberty was acutely grateful that this was being looked into, given the initial case had not belonged to this police department. "I wouldn't want to get you into any sort of trouble on my account."

This was certainly a far cry from the gung-ho detective who had come storming into his squad room yesterday, demanding cooperation, Campbell couldn't help thinking.

"Think of it as a joint project. Lieutenant Trask doesn't like serial killers any more than the rest of us do," Campbell told her. "But don't worry, this investigation has already been sanctioned by the powers that be."

"By God?" she asked whimsically as she continued labeling folders with the names of the victims.

"In a manner of speaking, I guess you could say yes," he answered. Then, to be perfectly clear, he clarified, "It's the Chief of D's."

"You ran this past the chief of detectives?" she asked, surprised.

When had he had the opportunity to do that? She had only brought the case to him yesterday and he hadn't appeared to be that taken by her request to begin with. The detective, she couldn't help thinking, was full of surprises.

"Well, not personally," Campbell admitted as he

wrote down a few notes to himself as he prepared to get his partner to delve into the victims.

She didn't understand. How did the Chief of D's become involved? "Then—"

"Let's just say that nothing stays secret in the police department. News around here travels *very* fast." He summed it up for her because she was still looking at him quizzically. "The minute you walked in and stated the reason for your visit to Aurora, theories began to spring up."

"Wow," was all she could say. Liberty shook her head, stunned. "And I thought news traveled fast in a small town."

Tickled, Campbell laughed. "A small town's got *nothing* on us," he assured her. "We're close-knit and closemouthed when we have to be—and *only* when we have to be. The rest of the time..." His voice trailed off. "I'm going to go get Choi. You pick the names of the people you want to work up from that list you brought with you, and Choi and I will take the others," Campbell told Liberty as he left the room.

She had a good feeling about this. For the first time in a very long time, Liberty was actually feeling hopeful.

Although she didn't realize it, she was smiling when Campbell came back into the conference room. Choi was right behind him.

"You're smiling," Campbell noted. "You find something?"

"Yes," she answered. Before he could ask her what she had found, she told him. "Hope."

He understood immediately and was happy that she had found something positive to hang on to. He had always been a firm believer that everyone needed to have hope in their lives, especially at the lowest moments.

"Good," Campbell said, pulling out one of the chairs and dropping into it. "Let's work with that."

Although they divided the names among themselves, the task didn't get any easier. Finding the necessary information was a challenge, even in this age of endless access.

Some of the victims had very little information noted on any data bank. Those names were put to the side, earmarked for more extensive searches later. In the meantime, Campbell, Liberty and Choi compiled what information they could and noted it beneath the names of the victims on the bulletin board.

By five o'clock, the list of people to contact for nineteen of the victims had in some cases grown extensively. The other eleven victims would necessitate more in-depth research.

"I don't know about you guys," Choi said, scrubbing his hands over his face and stifling a yawn, although not all too successfully. "But I'm going to call it a night." He glanced at the list he had printed out next to his computer. "All in all, I think we did some pretty good work." Campbell's partner glanced in Liberty's direction. "What about you?" he asked the visiting detective.

"Well, it's a start," she said with a nod. And then, abruptly, Liberty realized that she probably had sounded ungrateful about all the effort that had gone into this afternoon's work. "But it's a good one," she added, flashing Choi a smile.

"Don't mind her," Campbell told his partner. "She's happier than she sounds. Arizona tends to get really caught up in things to the point that she's wearing blinders when it comes to anything else."

"I said it was a good start," Liberty pointed out.

"And we all know you mean that," Campbell told her.

To Liberty, it still sounded as if Campbell was just humoring her, attempting to placate her. But then, maybe she was rather tired. She felt like her nerves had been stretched almost beyond their maximum endurance.

"You know," Campbell said, putting down the pen he had been using to make notes to himself, "I think this would be a good place for a break."

Preoccupied, Liberty absently asked, "For the hour?" In her head, she was already making plans on what she wanted to look into after dinner.

"No." Campbell corrected her misunderstanding. "For the night."

"That's definitely my cue to leave," Choi said, rising. And then the homicide detective looked at the two people at the table. "The kids don't like watching Mommy and Daddy fight."

"Nobody's fighting, Choi," Campbell told his partner patiently.

"Right." The detective glanced from his partner to the visiting detective. "Give it a few minutes," Choi replied under his breath. "I'll see you two in the morning. Me, I've got a less than happy wife to appease."

Liberty was not about to just walk away. Maybe they could order in and continue working. She tried to get him to focus on that agenda by asking Campbell as cheerfully as possible, "When would you like to get back to work?"

"Tomorrow morning." There was no arguing with the tone he used.

Undaunted, Liberty decided to give it one last shot. She looked at him, her eyes all but silently pleading with him. "Then that's it?"

There was a large, old-fashioned clock hanging on the rear wall of the conference room. Campbell jerked his thumb at it for emphasis. "I'd hardly call an almost ten-hour day 'it.' All in all, we've all worked pretty hard today."

She did what she could to harness the sudden, final blast of energy she felt threatening to run amok within her. Taking a deep breath, she collected herself. "You're right. I would have never expected to get this far on my own. And I know I have you to thank for that. If I seem to sound as if I'm being ungrateful, I'm definitely not. It's just that I've never gotten this far before and I don't want to stop because part of me is afraid that it'll somehow all disappear by morning."

He was looking at her as if she were crazy, so Liberty tried to explain. "You know, like Cinderella, fleeing from the ball at midnight just before the horses turned back into mice and the coach turned back into a pumpkin right under her."

"Nobody's turning into mice or pumpkins, Arizona." He gestured toward the monitors. "All this will keep until morning. However, you might turn into mush if you keep pushing yourself this way. So, in the interest of keeping you from self-destructing, I'm going to make you eat dinner."

"You're not planning on cooking again, are you?" she asked. After the full day he had put in, that made her feel more than a little guilty. And she definitely wasn't up to making an attempt herself.

"Nope, not me," he told her.

"Are we getting takeout? Or going to a restaurant?" she asked when he didn't say yes to her takeout question.

"We are going to Chez Andrew," Campbell told her whimsically.

"Is that the name of a restaurant?" Liberty asked. It wasn't a name she was familiar with, but then, she reminded herself, there were a lot of those around.

"No. That's the name of one of my uncles," he told her. "The family patriarch, as a matter of fact."

She stared at him wide-eyed. "You're making the poor man cook for us?"

Campbell laughed. He was going to have to remember this story to tell Andrew. "One does not 'make' Uncle Andrew cook. One cannot 'stop' the man from cooking. One can only get out of his way when he gets started whipping up meals. My uncle, the former chief of police, by the way, can call together a family gathering at the drop of a spatula. He uses food as a form of bribery to get the family together," he confided with a very large grin. "And when I told him about your investigation, he expressed a desire to meet you. For him, that involves making you dinner."

"He doesn't have to make me anything," Liberty stressed.

"Would you actually deny the man the pleasure of serving you one of his meals?" Campbell asked.

She stared at Campbell. "You're serious?" she asked. Liberty was having a great deal of trouble wrapping her mind around the very idea of a man actually *wanting* to prepare a meal for a perfect stranger prior to meeting her.

"Yes, I'm serious," he told her. "Nobody kids about Uncle Andrew's meals. When he retired from the force to take care of his kids, he took up cooking as a way of easing his tension. In very short order, it became his passion."

But something else Campbell had said had caught her attention. "Why did he have to take care of his kids?"

"That is a long story. One I'm sure he'd love to tell you over dinner—" Campbell glanced up at the clock on the wall "—which should be ready any minute now. So I suggest we get going."

Dumbfounded again, Liberty could only stare at Campbell as he led her away.

Chapter 11

The moment the front door of the recently renovated two-story house opened, Liberty was enveloped by warm, delicious, tempting smells. Smells that triggered the thought that this was what family was all about.

It was like walking into a Norman Rockwell painting. The sight made her think of all those stories she used to weave in her head whenever she would pretend that she was someone else and not the orphan in secondhand clothing going from one home to another.

When she was very young, Liberty used to think that the people who ran child services were trying to lose her, hoping someone would just misplace her. It was only by accident that she wound up living with Florence. The nurse had turned out to be the best thing that ever happened to her.

Along with the wonderful aroma that swirled around her, Liberty found herself looking at a silver-haired, muscular man who brought the phrase "larger than life" to mind. She would have judged him to be in his late sixties and fitter looking than a lot of men she encountered who were much younger.

The man knew how to take care of himself, she thought.

"You must be Liberty," Andrew Cavanaugh greeted her in a deep, warm voice that, like the aroma permeating throughout his home, all but engulfed her.

"I must be," Liberty replied even as she silently upbraided herself for uttering such a lame response.

"Well, come in, come in," Andrew said, urging her as well as his nephew into his house. "I hope that you're hungry."

"She hasn't eaten much the whole day, Uncle Andrew, so I'd say that was a pretty safe bet," Campbell said, walking in behind her.

Andrew nodded knowingly. "I know what that's like. You get so caught up in your work, you forget to eat, or even drink anything. But you can only do that for so long."

At that moment, a very attractive older woman with silver streaks in her mostly blond hair came out to join them. She flashed a sunny smile at both visitors.

"You're right on time," she told them. "Andrew's pot roast is ready to serve. I have no idea how he does that," she confided. "The man just cooks rings around me. But then, he always has. I found that disconcerting when we were first married," she told them, then added with a wide smile, "But now I love it."

Andrew easily slipped his arm around the woman's waist. "Liberty, allow me to introduce you to the love of my life, my wife, Rose." He turned toward Rose, pressing a kiss to her temple. "Darling, this is the young detective from Arizona that Brian was telling us about. Liberty Lawrence."

Andrew's words caught Liberty off guard. "The chief of detectives told you about me?" she asked. Maybe he was referring to another Brian.

"I just refer to him as my little brother," Andrew said with a chuckle. "But yes, for all intents and purposes, he is the Chief of D's."

Liberty looked at the former police chief uncertainly. "But I don't remember meeting him," she protested.

"You didn't," Andrew told her. "At least, not face to face, to my knowledge. But Brian has a way of taking in things quickly. Even if he's just passing by. And he always makes sure he gets filled in on details that are important to him. Between you and me—" Andrew leaned in a little closer "—I think he reads minds."

Rose looked over her shoulder into the family room. "Dinner's on the table, Andrew," his wife prompted.

"Yes, and it's getting cold as I speak," he guessed. "Yes, I know." He turned on his heel and led the way to the next room. "Please, follow me to the family room. I thought we'd eat there. It's cozier."

That was the word for it, Liberty thought, getting

her first glance into the room as she walked behind the former police chief.

And then she stopped dead in her tracks. There, in the middle of the room, stood a giant twelve-foot tree, almost completely decorated.

“You have your Christmas tree up,” she noted in surprise.

“Yes, it goes up the first of December,” Brian told her proudly. “The way I see it, with all the time it takes to put up the decorations, we might as well enjoy it for the entire Christmas season.”

For a few seconds, Liberty felt like the kid she had never been, not until the day she’d come to live with Florence.

“It’s very impressive,” she finally told her host and hostess.

“You like it?” Andrew asked, pleased. “Feel free to come over any time while you’re in Aurora. Our door’s always open to anyone working with members of the family,” he told her. “You can even help out with the decorating. As you can see—” he gestured toward the tree “—it’s not done yet.”

“He means that, you know,” Campbell said. “Both about the decorating and about just coming over.”

“Of course I mean it,” Andrew said. “I was taught never to say anything I didn’t mean.” He glanced at his wife. “Right, Rose?”

“I can definitely attest to that,” Rose told Liberty with a nod.

Andrew smiled at his wife. “All right, everyone, dig in. Please,” he urged, gesturing at the pot roast with its array of four different vegetables surrounding it. "And later, when we're finished, if you want to hang a few ornaments, you can take your pick," he told Liberty.

"We haven't quite finished decorating the tree. With all the members of the family involved, it's a never-ending process," Rose told their guest as she sat at the table. "So feel free to pitch in later."

"I don't think you'll have to twist her arm, Aunt Rose," Campbell said. He had caught the wistful expression on Liberty's face.

"I've just never seen a tree that big," Liberty confessed. "Just how big is it?"

"It's a twelve-footer," Andrew told her.

Rose smiled. "Andrew believes in doing things in a big way." She looked over at her husband. "Hence the large family."

"You can't blame that all on me," Andrew protested. "My father, Seamus, and his late brother, Murdoch, were responsible for starting that," he explained. "My father had four sons. Murdoch had three sons as well as a daughter."

"And they all went forth and multiplied," Campbell quipped.

"Say, why don't I have a family gathering?" Andrew suggested, saying it as if the idea had just occurred to him for the first time rather than with a fair amount of regularity. "That way, you can meet most of the family and we can also finish decorating Rose's tree."

"He calls it that because the first time he bought

the giant tree," Campbell told Liberty, "it was to celebrate the year he found Aunt Rose."

"You mean when they got married?" Liberty asked, not completely following what Campbell was telling her.

"No, Campbell means when Andrew finally found me." Rose saw the perplexed look on Liberty's face. "Long story," she said. "And you didn't come here for that. You came for some of Andrew's cooking and to talk about the case that brought you here."

"That's my girl," Andrew said affectionately. "Always cutting to the heart of the matter." He looked at the two people at his table. "Why don't we eat, then we can discuss the case you two are working? And I'll help in any way I can," he promised, although to his way of thinking, that went without saying.

Campbell smiled at the family patriarch. "Sounds like a good deal to me," he said and then amended as he glanced toward Liberty. "To us." After all, she had been the one to bring his attention to the fact that the cases appeared to be connected.

In the end, Liberty left the Cavanaugh house full and she also left with a great deal of confidence that with enough patience and help, she would be able to track down the vicious serial killer.

Andrew Cavanaugh was more than partially responsible for that feeling once she heard the full story behind what he had meant by his "finding Rose."

Apparently, the couple had had an argument and, atypically, Rose had driven off in a huff. That one angry incident had been the cause behind eleven years of grief. In her anger, Rose hadn't paid attention to where she was going. It was raining hard, and Rose wound up driving off the road and into the lake.

The car had been found the next day, but no matter how much they'd looked, no one had found any sign of her body. Eventually they'd given up and everyone advised the then police chief to move on.

But Andrew had stubbornly refused.

In the years that followed, Andrew had never given up hope that his wife was out there somewhere, alive. After a while, he'd taken early retirement to take care of and raise his five children. Every so often, he would get a lead and did his best to follow it up, but always to no avail.

It wasn't until his youngest, Rayne, following up on a case north of Aurora, had stopped at a diner that life had suddenly taken a turn for the better. Rayne could have sworn that the waitress who'd served her looked like an older version of her mother's photograph. When she'd come home and told Andrew about it, he'd lost no time in checking the story out.

The waitress had turned out to be his wife, except she hadn't known it. Because of the nature of the accident she had suffered—her car going off the road into the lake—she'd sustained amnesia. She'd had no memory of what had happened to her before she'd crawled out of the lake.

A good Samaritan had found her and taken her to a hospital. She'd built her life up from there.

Andrew had managed to convince her to come

back with him to Aurora. He'd patiently tried to reintroduce her to her old life. But it wasn't until an incident with a faulty shower head that sprayed her in the face with a torrent of water that Rose's whole life had suddenly come flashing back to her.

The upshot of that was, Andrew told her, if you believe in something, you don't have the right to give up until you finally manage to make it happen.

Liberty left, totally impressed.

"No offense, Campbell, but I think I love your uncle," she told the detective on the way home.

"None taken," Campbell assured her with a laugh. "Most everyone I know feels that way about him to some degree. Uncle Andrew is pretty damn terrific. Nobody else I know would have been able to continue searching for his wife after all that time. And the best part is that it finally paid off."

"Yes," she agreed quietly. "It did." The story had filled her with excitement as well as energy. "There's no chance of us going back to the police station tonight, is there?"

"Tomorrow," Campbell told her. "We haven't gotten enough in to be able to determine the guy's identity, so there's no point in running back there tonight, Arizona. Uncle Andrew would be the first one to tell you to get your rest so you can get a fresh start in the morning. Maybe by then, Valri will have gotten somewhere with the surveillance tape that we left for her to review."

She sighed. He was right. "So, back to your place?"

she asked, staring out the passenger window, watching the lights go by.

"Don't worry. I don't collect rent until the third week in," he said dryly. Then, in case she thought he was being serious, Campbell told her, "I'm just kidding, Arizona. You're welcome to stay as long as you'd like. And, like I said the other day, if my place doesn't suit you, there are a lot of people in my family who would willingly take you in."

Hard as it was for her to fathom, she was beginning to believe that, even though she had never come across people like his family before.

"Kind of the Cavanaugh version of musical beds, eh?" she asked.

Campbell laughed. "I suppose that's one way of looking at it. Another way to look at it is that we're a big law enforcement family and we always take care of our own."

"But I'm not part of your family," Liberty pointed out.

"It's all in how you look at it. There's 'family,'" Campbell told her, "and then there's *family*. In spirit," he underscored. "You qualify for the latter."

"Well—" She stifled a yawn. "You're lucky because I'm too tired to argue," Liberty admitted. "So, okay."

Campbell smiled, amused. "Knew I'd wind up wearing you down."

"Campbell?" Liberty said as he pulled into the carport.

"Yes?" he asked, getting out and coming around to her side in time to open the door for her. He watched, fascinated, as this ball of fire got out in what, for her, was slow motion. She had to be very tired.

"I really had a nice time tonight," she told him. "Thanks for taking me to meet your uncle and aunt."

"I had very little to do with it," he told her, locking the vehicle and then carefully steering her toward his second-floor apartment. "Uncle Andrew insisted on meeting you. I guess hearing about your determination to find that serial killer struck a chord for him."

For whatever reason, she was glad she'd gotten to hear the chief's story.

"That was a pretty inspiring love story when you get right down to it," Liberty said. "In all that time, your uncle never gave up hope of finding his wife alive. Anyone else would have moved on."

They were inside his apartment by then and she turned to Campbell as he closed the front door. "Thank you," she said.

And then, she surprised them both by punctuating the two words with a deep, heartfelt kiss.

It just happened without warning, astonishing both of them. One moment she was thanking him for the evening, for the story, for *everything.* The next moment, she was kissing him. It was hard to say who was more surprised.

Or who enjoyed it more.

She jolted, stepping back as if suddenly realizing what was happening. And that it shouldn't be.

"I'm sorry," she apologized, stunned at what she had just done. The words rang hollow in her ears. "I didn't mean to do that."

"I was kind of hoping that you did." She looked like a deer unexpectedly caught in the headlights, and Campbell found himself searching to put her at ease. "Don't worry," he told her, "I'm not about to follow up on what just happened." Although, he would have liked nothing better than to do just that. He could still taste her on his lips. "I realize that you're tired and not thinking clearly, and I'm not the kind of guy to push himself on a woman."

She still eyed him uncertainly.

"Even if I were so inclined, I've got sisters and cousins—and a few brothers—who would skin me alive if I even so much as *tried* to follow up on that," he said. "And, if you're the slightest bit concerned, you've got that lock on the *inside* of the bedroom door that I know you've already tested out. See you first thing in the morning, Arizona," he told her, turning away and heading toward his own bedroom.

As he walked away, Campbell pressed his lips together. He could *still* taste her.

A warm, tempting feeling shifted through him. For just a second, Campbell allowed his mind to drift. But then he deliberately blocked any further thoughts about the woman from his mind. There was nothing to be gained by going that route. She was here trying to find a serial killer who had taken the life of someone important to her. He couldn't allow his own feelings to get in the way of that.

Later, when this was over—*if* it was ever going to be over—there was time enough to pursue this other avenue to its most likely end.

But until then, he had to keep his mind focused on the prize—which was *not* the sexy visiting detective down the hall.

At least, he thought, it wasn't the prize *yet*.

Chapter 12

Despite hardly being able to keep her eyes open, Liberty didn't really sleep well that night.

The entire time, every time she did fall asleep, she kept having recurring dreams about Campbell.

Not only that, but she had dreams about her foster mother as well. Throughout, the dreams were interspersed with moments that highlighted the very short contact of her lips on his.

In addition, even in her dreams, Liberty was acutely aware of the fact that she had been the one to initiate the kiss and not the other way around.

Consequently, when morning finally came, she felt as if she was more exhausted than when she had initially gone to bed.

She really hoped that if Campbell noticed that she

looked less than bright-eyed and bushy-tailed, despite her artful application of makeup, he would have the good grace not to mention that fact.

Moreover, she hoped that his silence would extend to his *not* saying anything about that misstep of hers last night.

That was the only way she could think to refer to her having given in to an impulse and kissed him, although, in the absolute sense, she really didn't think of what she had done as a misstep but more of an accident.

The more she relived it, the more right it seemed—although there was no way she would ever admit that to Campbell.

Bracing herself, Liberty walked into his kitchen, prepared to see Campbell at the stove, making breakfast just like yesterday. However, it appeared that breakfast was on hold.

Campbell was on the phone, obviously talking to someone he knew. He seemed exceedingly serious. She mentally crossed her fingers and hoped that this was about the case and not about something else.

"All right, I'll be right there," Campbell said into his cell phone just before he terminated the call.

Liberty waited until he put his phone away before she made her presence known to him.

Clearing her throat, she prompted, "You caught a case that's taking you away."

Campbell turned around to face her. If he was surprised to see her standing there, he didn't show it. "Not 'away' in the sense that you mean," he answered.

"Catching this serial killer just became a top priority. He just killed another nurse. Some homeless guy just found her body in a dumpster while foraging for his breakfast. According to the medical examiner on the scene, the poor guy threw up what little food he had in his stomach," Campbell said sympathetically as he thought to turn off the burner beneath his frying pan.

Breakfast forgotten, Liberty was eager to get going. She crossed the kitchen to the tiny foyer and picked up the purse she had put there.

"Okay, let's go!" she urged.

Campbell glanced at the frying pan. "Don't you want anything for breakfast?" he asked.

Doubling back, she picked up the two slices of toast he had placed on the plate sitting at her place setting on the table.

"Got it," Liberty declared. "Now let's go," she repeated. And then she thought that maybe he wanted to have breakfast himself. "Or, you can meet me at the squad room when you're done."

"Hold your horses, Arizona," he called out. "I'm coming with you. Just wait for me to pack up a few things," Campbell told her.

"I don't want to interrupt your breakfast," she protested, one hand already on the doorknob, twisting it open.

She made him think of a racehorse pawing on the ground at the starting gate.

"I already ate," he told her. "This is for you." He nodded at the contents of the pan. "I made this western omelet for you and I'll be damned if it's going to be left behind." Campbell emptied the pan and wrapped the contents in foil. "You can nibble on it while we work."

Liberty had been slightly hungry when she'd come down, but the minute Campbell had told her that yet another body had been found, that completely nullified her appetite. Still, she had to admit that she was touched by his thoughtfulness. Moreover, she definitely didn't want to insult him.

"Thanks." She took the foil-wrapped offering from him as she flashed a smile at Campbell. "Does the victim fit the profile?" she queried as she followed the detective out the door.

Locking the door, he headed for the carport. "Yes. She was a nurse and about thirty-five, which puts her in the right age bracket. And the killer used the same weapon. Piano wire," he told her. "But there was a difference this time."

He had her complete attention. "Oh? What was the difference?"

"The victim wasn't wearing scrubs," he told her as he pulled out of the complex. "She was dressed up, as if she was going out for the evening."

Liberty's heart skipped a beat. They were getting closer, she could *feel* it. "You think she found him on a dating site," she asked Campbell. "Like the last victim?" It sounded as if the killer was upping his game.

"I don't know. That's for her friends or family to tell us," Campbell suggested.

Since she had first begun exploring this connection, there was one question Liberty had shied away from asking or even thinking about. But she had never been the type to stick her head in the sand, either, even though she really didn't want to think about this possibility because of her foster mother.

Liberty knew it had to be faced sooner or later. "Was she violated?" she asked Campbell.

"They obviously hadn't done a thorough autopsy yet, but in his initial exam, the medical examiner didn't find anything to suggest that the victim had been raped," Campbell told her.

While she was grateful the victims might have been spared that ultimate degradation, in a way, that also cut down on the possibility the killer might have slipped up. If he didn't violate his victims, then that was one less way he would have left behind some of his DNA, she thought. DNA that could ultimately lead to making an identification.

"It's been less than a week between the two murders," Campbell pointed out. "That means that the killer is escalating." He took a left turn at the end of the block as he headed for the crime scene. "That also means that somewhere along the line, he's going to get sloppy. And when he does," he said, sparing Liberty a significant glance, "that's when we'll get him, Arizona. We'll get the SOB."

Liberty nodded, almost too afraid to hope. But then, hope was all she had.

They arrived at the scene of the latest murder. The area at the rear of the restaurant had been roped off. Foot traffic at that hour of the morning was rare and the people who were out walking stayed clear of it. The idea that an actual murder had taken place so close to their own homes genuinely upset and unsettled them, although there were a couple of stragglers milling around, craning their necks to catch a glimpse of the body.

But the victim had already been placed in a body bag and loaded onto a gurney, so there wasn't much to see, Liberty thought, looking around as Campbell pulled his car up in the restaurant's parking lot.

The homeless man who had found the body was sitting on the steps of the ambulance that had been called in. A paramedic was checking him out. The homeless man was exceedingly pale, the shock of discovering the body imprinted on his face.

Making his way over to the man, Campbell said to the paramedic, "Give us a few minutes."

"I can give you the rest of the day—he checks out okay," he said, putting away the instruments he had used on the homeless man. "By the way, he says his name is Jake 'Smith' and I think that ghostly white is his natural color."

At that moment, Jake made eye contact with Liberty and she smiled at him.

In a way, Liberty felt a kinship with the homeless man. In her own way, she reasoned, she had been homeless, too, and she had definitely felt that same emptiness he had to be experiencing right now.

As Campbell introduced himself to Jake, preparing to ask him what he might have noticed when he stumbled across the dead nurse, Liberty dug into her purse. She took out two twenties and handed it to the homeless man. Jake looked up at her as if she were some sort of angel sent his way in answer to a prayer.

"Get yourself something to eat," she told him. "That must have been a terrible shock for you this morning."

Jake nodded his head as he shivered in agreement. "I'll say," he mumbled in response.

"When you found the body," Campbell gently prompted, "did you happen to see anything or anyone in the general area?"

Jake shook his head. "Just her," he answered, the words coming out in a single breath. "She had this wire around her neck, it was pulled really tight. She wasn't expecting it," Jake added after a beat, shivering at the memory.

"How do you know that?" Campbell asked.

"By the look on her face," Jake answered. And then he shook his head. "It was awful. That look is going to haunt me for the rest of my life," he told them, shivering again.

"And you're sure you didn't see anyone milling about?" Campbell persisted.

Jake shook his head again. "Nobody to see," he told the two people listening to his story. "I always wait until there's nobody around before I go through the dumpster behind a restaurant. Having me foraging through what a place like that throws away isn't exactly good for their image."

"Understood." They were done for now, Campbell thought. He reached into his pocket and took out a card. Making sure it was the right one, he offered the card to Jake.

"This is the name of a homeless shelter in the area. You'll be able to get a hot meal there and a clean bed for the night, or however long you want to stay. They can also help you find a job if you want one," he told Jake, watching the homeless man's face to see if that caught his attention.

Jake stared at the card in his hand for a long moment and then pocketed it before handing Liberty back the money she had given him.

Surprised, she looked at him quizzically.

"If I'm gonna go to the mission, I guess I should give this back to you," Jake told her almost shyly.

Liberty shook her head, pushing his hand away. "You keep that," she told Jake. "You never know when you might need it."

For the second time since he had met her a few short minutes ago, Jake looked totally astonished. For a moment, he didn't look as if he knew what to say. And then, stumbling over his own tongue, he managed to thank her. Profusely.

Meanwhile, Campbell was scanning the area for one of the patrol officers he knew was on the premises.

"Hey, Rafferty, do me a favor and drive Jake here over to the homeless shelter on Winfred. Tell them he needs a place to stay for a few days. If they need any further explanation, have them call me."

"That was very nice of you," Liberty commented to Campbell as the officer took Jake to his vehicle.

"I could say the same thing about you and that money you gave him. Most people give a couple of bucks, if they give anything at all," Campbell told her.

"There's not much you can buy for a couple of bucks these days," Liberty said. "Referring him to a homeless shelter that can connect him to a hot meal, as well as a possible job, is the far more hopeful way to go."

Campbell wasn't about to make too much of that just yet and he said as much to her. "You can lead a man to water, but you can't make him drink."

She glanced over to where the officer was putting Jake into his vehicle. "Oh, I have this feeling that Jake is going to be more than happy to drink that water," Liberty told him. And then, rolling the comment over in her head, she laughed. "I guess that some of your optimism is finally rubbing off on me."

"Nice to know," he told her. "Let's find out if Choi managed to get the restaurant owner to come in."

Campbell circled around the building, making his way to the restaurant's front door. He continued with his narrative for Liberty's benefit.

"Choi gave the man a choice of coming in early to talk to us, or going down to the precinct." He looked in through the glass door to see how the situation had gone. There was a heavy-set man inside, looking less than happy as he talked to Campbell's partner. "Looks like the owner decided that coming in was the easier choice," he told Liberty.

"The guy's not overly thrilled about either choice, but this was the better way to go," Choi told his partner as he pushed open the front door to admit Campbell and Liberty. He guessed at the topic under discussion. "As a matter of fact, brace yourself."

"Why?" Liberty asked.

"Because the owner is clearly a wreck," Choi confided.

"My guess is he's probably afraid that this is going to affect his business adversely," Campbell said. "After all, he does own the restaurant, right?"

"Right," Choi agreed then added, "Well, it's certainly not exactly good for business." And then realizing how that must have sounded to Liberty because of her connection to one of the serial killer's victims, Choi flushed. "Sorry, no offense intended," he told her.

She appreciated the apology and knew that Choi's comment hadn't really meant anything. "None taken, Detective."

Coming into the heart of the restaurant, they saw the distraught owner. Alan Baker looked as if he was going to go all to pieces any moment now. His deep brown eyes appeared as if they were about to fall right out of his head as he glanced from one detective to the next and then back again.

When he spoke, Baker sounded as if he was on the verge of hysteria. "How could this have happened?" he demanded, his voice all but cracking.

"That's what we're attempting to find out, sir," Campbell said to the man who appeared to be envisioning financial disaster waiting to leap out and grab him by the throat.

Campbell's response didn't seem to placate the owner. "This is a high-end restaurant in one of the safest cities in the entire country," Baker all but wailed. His unspoken question was clear. Why had something like his happened here?

"We know that, sir," Campbell told the owner patiently. "If we could get a look at your surveillance tapes from last night, specifically from the camera that's facing the alley where your dumpster is located, we might be able to clear up at least some of that mystery for all of us."

"I can take you to the room where the monitors are all kept," Baker told the police detectives, still looking distressed. "But I really don't know the first thing about extracting any information off those tapes." Realizing how that had to have sounded, he quickly explained why. "There're just too many details involved in running a restaurant this size. I leave these minor details to my security guard while I tackle the bigger things."

Campbell wasn't about to attempt to stroke the man's ego and make him feel better about the way he handled things. "And where is your security guard?"

Baker looked at the front door, as if willing the guard to materialize. He didn't. "He doesn't come in until we open up," Baker explained after a beat. "I could try calling him, but he's usually hard to reach. The calls go to his voicemail. He does good work when he's here."

"Try calling him anyway," Campbell instructed.

"That's okay," Liberty told Campbell, speaking up. "Don't bother. I know how to load the tapes and cue them up," she told the other two detectives. She had already done that at the first crime scene the other day. This should be no different. "Just take me to the surveillance room."

Both Campbell and Choi appeared pleased. However, for the first time, the owner looked rather doubtful. "Well, I don't know..."

"Look," Choi said, finally adding his two cents to the discussion. "It's either let Detective Lawrence here view the tapes, or we bundle the tapes *and* you up and take both of you to the precinct. Your choice, Mr. Baker," he said, looking at the owner pointedly.

It didn't take Baker long to make up his mind. "They're kept right in here," the owner said, leading the way to the back room.

"Need any help?" Campbell offered, looking at Liberty once they got to the room. There were several monitors lined up, one next to the other. All in all, it looked like a rather daunting undertaking.

"I've got this," Liberty assured him. "Why don't you and Choi see if Baker or any of his staff has any information they're not aware of knowing."

That, Liberty mused, turned out to be the case more often than anyone would have thought possible.

"What?" Choi asked, looking at Liberty, clearly bewildered.

"I know what she means," Campbell told his partner.

Choi shrugged. "That makes one of us," he

murmured, following his partner out of the small, cramped room.

Liberty hardly heard him. She was already busy reviewing the tapes.

Chapter 13

As Liberty sat, carefully reviewing all the surveillance videos from not only the alley, but also from within the actual restaurant, Campbell and Choi were busy questioning the restaurant workers. That included all the servers as well as the kitchen staff, all of whom the owner had been told to call in.

They'd all come in, some looking rather leery and nervous because the story about the strangling victim discovered behind their restaurant had already hit the news.

Questioning the staff ultimately led nowhere. To a worker, no one had seen anything that appeared to be the least bit suspicious. But then Campbell really hadn't thought they would have, otherwise someone might have come forward by now.

Still, he thought, there was always that outside chance, so he'd been bound to give it a try.

Finished questioning the last staff member, Campbell and Choi left the owner's office where they had been conducting the interrogations.

"Let's hope Arizona was more successful than we were," Campbell said to his partner.

"Well, I really doubt that there was any way she could have been less successful," Choi remarked, following Campbell down the hallway.

Knocking on the security room door, Campbell popped his head in. He fully expected to find Liberty frowning and murmuring under her breath—or, depending on her level of frustration, vocally threatening to drop kick one of the monitors.

"Anything?" he asked her, trying not to pin too much hope into his tone.

"Something," she responded.

That caught Campbell's attention, as well as surprised him. "You're kidding. Really?" Campbell came into the room, closely followed by his partner. It was a tight squeeze, but Campbell hardly noticed. He was focused on the monitor Liberty was looking at. "What?" he asked. "What did you find?"

Glancing at Choi to see if his partner saw anything, the latter merely shook his head and shrugged.

Liberty rewound the tape and then cued it to the portion that had caught her attention.

"Does this guy look familiar to you?" she asked, pointing out a dark-haired man walking away from the alley.

Campbell leaned over her, taking a closer look at the monitor. She did her best not to respond to the body heat she felt passing between them, but because of the intimacy her search managed to create, it wasn't easy.

Due to the camera angle, there was only a partial view of the area. Campbell shook his head. "No, should he?" he asked Liberty.

"I could swear he resembles that guy we saw pulling out of the parking lot in that previous murder you caught." To jog Campbell's memory, she said, "You know that clip containing that partial license plate that is currently with Valri," she told him. "All I know is that it looks like the same guy to me."

She turned to look at Campbell's face to see if the detective agreed.

"The blurry guy with no name," Choi suddenly recalled, making the connection.

Liberty flashed the other detective a smile. "One and the same," she acknowledged, pleased that Choi had picked up on it as well. "And there's something else," she told the two detectives. Rewinding the tape again, she paused a number frames before the shot she had just shown them, then hit Play.

"Notice anything?" she asked both men, looking from Campbell to Choi.

The partners watched the tape again. When neither detective responded to her question with an answer, she rewound the tape a third time.

This time Campbell was the first to notice it. How had he missed seeing it? he couldn't help wondering.

"Someone—or *something*—moved the surveillance camera a little to the left."

"Bingo," Liberty declared. "Give that man a cigar. Whoever did it—my guess is that's it our serial killer—made sure he remained out of camera range while he repositioned the camera in order to dump the body without being seen."

"You want to get the forensic team out here to check the camera for any possible prints they might find?" Choi asked his partner.

"Probably a waste of time," Campbell told him. "If the guy's smart enough to reposition the camera, he's smart enough not to leave behind any prints for us to find. But it still wouldn't hurt to have them go over everything—just in case." He paused briefly. "In the meantime, we need to get a copy of that tape and have Valri follow up on it as well. Maybe if she compares this one with the one from the other restaurant, she can get some decent facial recognition—even if we don't have a name yet."

Liberty nodded. "Which of you gentlemen wants to ask the owner if we can borrow the tape?" she asked the detectives. "Since I'm the one who did the viewing? By the way, remind me to stop and get some eye drops on the way back to the station," she told Campbell. "I feel like my eyes are tread-worn—and dry enough to probably catch fire."

"Now there's something I wouldn't want to see," Campbell commented. He nodded toward the video machine. "Pop the tape and bring it with us."

She did as he requested then handed the cassette to

Campbell. "But you do the asking as per our agreement."

"I don't recall any agreement. Do you recall any agreement, Choi?" he asked his partner innocently.

It was obvious by the latter's expression that he didn't care for being caught in the middle of this, but since his loyalty was with Campbell, he said, "Nope, I don't."

"That's okay, I recall for all three of us," Liberty informed the other two detectives cheerfully. She placed her hands on Campbell's back and tactfully pushed the man out of the tiny room. "All right, let's get moving, Cavanaugh."

A wry smile curved Campbell's mouth. "I'm beginning to understand why that tiny town of yours had no objections sending you out here and away from them, Arizona. They probably felt that they all needed the break."

"Just keep moving, Cavanaugh," Liberty instructed.

"You know, you two should insist on a cover charge for the show," Choi told them, looking amused as he shook his head.

"We come bearing gifts, Valri," Campbell said as he and Liberty walked into the computer lab less than an hour later. Choi had temporarily left them to follow up, while Campbell and Liberty went to see Valri, on another lead they'd managed to uncover.

The two detectives were both hoping she had made some sort of progress with the tape they had left with her. In addition, they wanted to bring this newest one to her.

Valri sighed patiently at Campbell's reference to bearing gifts. "Why am I not surprised?" she said, looking up at her visitors.

"Because you're every bit as smart as you are beautiful," Campbell told her.

Valri made a long-suffering noise under her breath as she gave him an eye roll. "You're spreading it a bit thick, Cam."

"Ah, but I mean every word of it," Campbell told his cousin cheerfully. "Okay, cutting to the chase, have you gotten anywhere with facial recognition yet?"

"Unfortunately, no. I did manage to enhance the guy's likeness, but even so, I can't seem to find a match, which means either he has no record at all, or this guy is a master of disguises."

"Which way are you leaning?" Liberty asked the woman she already regarded as a computer wizard.

"Well, it is possible that he has no record," Valri said. "A lot of serial killers do elude being caught for an inordinate amount of time."

"But none of them had you on their 'trail,' so to speak," Campbell pointed out.

Valri rolled her eyes again. "Go back into your corner, Cam. I'll let you know if I find anything to actually go on."

Campbell nodded. "Fair enough," he told his cousin then turned toward Liberty. "I believe that we've just been given our cue to leave. Valri doesn't like having any witnesses around when she works her magic."

"If I could work magic," Valri informed the detective, "I'd find a way to turn you into another cousin."

"Another cousin?" Campbell said with an amused laugh. "Oh, face it, Val, you know we all drive you crazy to some degree or another. I've heard you say so more than once."

"Some accomplish that more than others," was the only comment Valri would allow herself to commit to, giving Campbell a telltale look. "Just remember, Cam, the longer I talk to you, the less time I have to focus on this." She waved her hand at her computer screen, which currently contained the likeness of the man driving away from the restaurant where Campbell's last victim had been discovered.

"We're already gone," Campbell told her. He looked over his shoulder at the detective from Arizona. The latter hadn't made a move to follow him out. "Aren't we, Arizona?" he prodded.

"Sure, whatever you say," Liberty responded, coming to.

He waited until they were out in the hallway. "Okay, what's on your mind?" he asked as they walked back to the elevator.

"What makes you think I have something on my mind?" Liberty asked.

"That's easy enough. You sound preoccupied," he told her. "Why? What gives?"

She pressed her lips together, thinking. "I'm just wondering why no bells went off."

She had lost him. "Any particular bells you're talking about?"

"From the looks of it, our serial killer was apparently on at least two dating sites."

"Okay?" he responded, waiting for her to make a point. He still didn't see why something like that would "ring bells."

"Well, don't you think it's rather off for our guy to be out on two dating sites to begin with. Wouldn't a low profile be more in keeping with his character?" she asked Campbell.

Campbell shrugged. "Maybe he was awkward and needed help," Campbell guessed. "I wouldn't know myself. But that was probably the story he told to get his victims to lower their guard. Also, reviewing the information on the dating site is a great way for him to hone in on nurses, since they seem to be his victim of choice."

"You have a point. Most likely, too, they took one look at our mystery man and probably felt as if they had hit the proverbial jackpot," Liberty commented grimly.

"Some jackpot," Campbell said.

"Hey, you're going in the wrong direction, Arizona," he called out to Liberty when she suddenly did a one-eighty and headed back to Valri's computer lab.

"No, I'm not." She tossed the words over her shoulder. "I've got an idea."

"Care to share?" he asked, quickening his gait as he followed her back to his cousin's lab.

"Sure," she answered. "You're welcome to come along."

Campbell blew out a breath. "I'm beginning to understand why you never had a partner. It wasn't that the town was so small, it was because no one would put up working with you."

"No comment," she responded "innocently."

By then, Liberty had reached the computer lab and, after a quick knock on the door, she went in.

Valri looked up. If she was surprised to see them, she hid it well.

"Twice in one day. Any reason why I'm so lucky today, Cam?"

"Ask her." He jerked his thumb in Liberty's direction. "She's the one who suddenly decided to make a beeline back to your office."

Liberty jumped in with an explanation. "Can you enhance that guy's photograph and print a copy for us to show around?"

"Sure. That's the easy part," Valri told her cousin's counterpart. "Give me a minute," she requested, hitting a few keys to get the photograph just right before printing a copy. Satisfied with the image on her computer, Valri hit Print. A faint noise was heard coming from another part of the lab, then ceased.

"I'll get it," Valri told them, getting up. Moving quickly, she retrieved the photograph and returned, holding it in her hand. "Will this do for your purposes?" she asked, raising the photograph in front of the Arizona detective.

"Perfect," Liberty told her. She lifted her eyes to

Valri's. "Do you think I could possibly have a few more copies?"

"You can have as many as you want. I can even make up a few wallet-sized ones. Starting a scrapbook?" she asked glibly.

"No, handing them out to however many detectives your cousin can get to, to try to track this guy down," Liberty answered.

"Okay, let's make it twenty—five—copies to start," Valri said. "Does that work for you?" she asked, looking at Campbell.

Campbell spread his hands, disavowing any opinion when it came to this. "Hey, apparently I'm just along for the ride. You two work it out," he told Valri good-naturedly.

"So, twenty-five copies to start okay with you?" Valri double-checked with Liberty before she finally typed in the number.

"Twenty-five will be just fine, Valri," Liberty agreed. "Besides, I can always come back here and ask the legendary wizard for more if the need arises, right?"

Valri smiled in response then regarded her cousin, who was standing off to the side. "I like her, Cam," she told him.

"Of course you do," he said dryly. "So, are we ready to go?" he asked Liberty. "Or is there something else you want to ask the wizard to give you before we leave?"

"I can think of one thing," she said, then immediately banished the thought from her mind. "But no, I think we're good for now." She took the pile of photographs that Valri handed her. "This'll help a lot," she assured the other woman.

"Whatever you need," Valri told her in all honesty. "I'm here to help."

"Hey, why don't you ever say that to me?" Campbell asked his cousin, pretending to be offended.

"You're family," Valri told him. "I don't have to be nice to you. Besides, you're used to abusing the privilege of being related to me. While she, on the other hand," Valri said, nodding at Liberty, "knows when not to cross the line and is nothing but polite when asking for something."

Campbell frowned. "You've known her for—what, a whole three days? Not even."

"Ah, but I'm a quick judge of character, not to mention a very good one," Valri pointed out.

"I think I need to get going," Campbell said, "before I'm tempted to commit whatever the proper term is for dressing down a cousin."

"If you find out, be sure to let me know, Cam," Valri called out after him as he and Liberty left the computer lab.

"Count on it," he promised just before he closed the door behind him.

Chapter 14

"Just why did you want so many copies of this guy's picture, Arizona?" Campbell asked the woman beside him as they walked down the hallway back to the elevator. "We don't even know for sure if he actually *is* the serial killer."

"Let's just say that I've got this gut feeling," Liberty answered.

Campbell laughed under his breath.

"What's so funny?" she asked.

"In my family, we're the ones who talk about having 'gut feelings,'" he told her.

Liberty nodded. "Well, maybe when it's your family, you do. But Florence was as close to family as I had," she told him. "As for the pictures, the worst thing that can happen is that the guy in the photo turns out *not* to be the guy we're after and we toss the photos. And if he *does* turn out to be our serial killer, then we'll have enough photos to blanket the entire area and everyone will be alerted to what he looks like," she told Campbell. "I find that people remember things more clearly if they have a photo to hang on to rather than just depend on their memories. And this way, if they happen to cross paths with this Romeo down the line, all they have to do is whip out the photo to make sure."

"I suppose that does have some merit," Campbell agreed.

Her mouth curved. She was surprised that he didn't want to argue with her about it. When they had initially met, he had struck her as someone who was willing to argue about *everything.*

She was gratified that he wasn't.

"Thank you for that," she told Campbell. "I know how much that had to cost you."

"Didn't cost me a thing," he told her in all innocence. "I'm open to anything. I just don't agree with everything I hear."

As they stood waiting for the elevator, Liberty spared him a glance. She had worked with visiting detectives in her hometown who acted as if they were the last word when it came to working theories. And they treated her as if she was just one step removed from a hayseed.

It was nice to discover he wasn't like that.

When she came right down to it, she had to admit that she liked their association. If nothing else, this was the first time she had entertained a measure of hope about finally being able to close in on the serial killer.

Liberty smiled at him. "Nice of you to admit that."

"This job is hard enough without posturing and bringing in egos." They got off the elevator. "What do you say we take those photos and run them past Cynthia's sister and her coworkers? Maybe it actually will jar someone's memory the way you hoped."

If only, Liberty thought. Out loud she told him, "Fingers crossed," as they went to the front entrance.

They went to the victim's place of work at the hospital first. Several of Cynthia's coworkers thought that they had noticed the man in the photograph somewhere on the premises, but on closer examination, they weren't really sure.

One of the nurses, Penelope Dixon, all but drooled over the photograph, apparently forgetting who the man in the photograph was supposed to represent.

"He really was a gorgeous guy," Penelope recalled. "I was tempted to sign up on that dating site myself—except I'm sure that my husband wouldn't be understanding about it." Penelope sighed wistfully. "But that is one delicious specimen of manhood."

And then, realizing what she had just said—and possibly about whom—she flushed, attempting to negate her words to Campbell. "At least Cynthia knew a little bit of joy before that terrible thing happened to her."

"Tell me, did you ever wonder why someone as

good-looking as this man appears to be needed to use a dating site before finding someone to go out with?" Campbell asked the nurse. He exchanged glances with Liberty and gave her a nod.

That was his way of giving her credit, Liberty thought, which meant that he really did buy into the theory she had advanced to him.

Another one of the day nurses who had worked with Cynthia, Sally Hopkins, added her two cents. "I just thought that Cynthia was the luckiest woman on the face of the earth—until that homicide detective came to inform us that she had been murdered." The nurse stared at the photo in her hand and frowned. "Is this the guy who did it?" Sally asked.

"We don't know yet," Campbell replied. "But he is a person of interest and we're trying to locate him in order to bring him in for questioning. Since capturing his partial likeness on camera, he seems to have disappeared from the face of the earth."

Sally looked at the photo again and released a heartfelt sigh. "Unless he's the killer, some woman might have snapped him up and taken him to her lair, unable to believe her good fortune."

"As for 'good fortune,' we'll reserve judgment on that," Liberty told the nurse. She flipped the photograph over for the woman's benefit. "Detective Cavanaugh's number and my number are on the back of the photo. If you or any of your friends happen to see this man, do not approach him. Please, just give Detective Cavanaugh or me a call."

"Absolutely," Sally replied. She glanced down at

the photograph. "I can keep this, right?" the nurse asked hopefully.

"Right," Campbell told her, sincerely hoping Liberty was correct about her "gut" feeling. They needed to close in on this killer before any other victims fell prey to this man's charms, the way these women apparently had.

They distributed several more photographs but, realistically, didn't think that they'd really managed to "jar" anyone's memory.

Their next stop was to go visit the victim's sister.

Liberty almost felt guilty because the woman looked so hopeful when she'd first seen them on her doorstep.

"Did you get him?" Judith cried.

"Not yet," Campbell told her. "But we haven't stopped working on it."

Liberty held up the photograph for the woman to view. "Do you, by any chance, recognize this man?"

Staring at the photograph, Judith turned completely pale. "Is he the one who killed Cynthia?" she asked, her voice sounding almost hollow and tinny.

"As I said, we don't know yet, but there *is* a slight possibility." And then Liberty had an idea. "Would it be possible for you to go through your sister's things for us?"

"I suppose," the woman replied warily. "What am I looking for?" she asked. "And I'm going to have to brace myself first. I have come to terms with never seeing her again."

She knew how that was, Liberty thought.

"It just occurred to us that there might be a chance that your sister could have made a copy of her date's picture from the actual dating app or site," Campbell suggested. Then he prompted, "You know, to show you once you got back from your vacation."

Cynthia's sister didn't seem to understand. "We were never in competition for men," she protested.

"I wasn't suggesting that there was a competition," Campbell told her. "Maybe she just wanted to share his picture with you, if things went well, because she was happy. And if this guy really does turn out to be the serial killer, he might have been camera shy—with apparently good reason, so she had to be clever about getting his picture to show you."

"And if she did make a copy off the website, then we'll have his bio—or his made-up bio," Liberty amended for the woman's benefit.

"The point is, we'll have a place to start," Campbell told the woman.

Judith set her mouth grimly. "I'll look through Cynthia's things," she promised. "Maybe I will find something," she said, looking at both detectives.

"It's a long shot," Campbell agreed, doing his best to be encouraging. "But you never know."

Liberty watched the woman pull back her shoulders, as if she were literally bracing herself for the ordeal.

"This might take some time," she warned the detectives.

"Because of the emotional cost?" Campbell suggested.

"No, because my sister was a semi-hoarder. Nothing overwhelming," she quickly assured them, not wanting to cast any sort of shadow on her sister. "She just never was able to get rid of any papers she thought were important in her life."

"Like the information about a potential date she pulled off the internet site?" Liberty asked hopefully.

The woman's eyes temporarily lit up. "Yes, like that."

"How do you do it?" Liberty asked Campbell once they were back in his car and driving to their next destination.

They had left Cynthia's sister to deal with the emotional task of sorting through what appeared to be ten years of papers, possibly more.

"I'm going to need more details, Arizona. How do I do what?" he asked. He hit a long stretch of road with sparse traffic, so he allowed himself a quick glance in Liberty's direction.

She took a deep breath, searching for patience as she answered. "How do you keep from screaming after going around in circles?"

"I'll let you in on a secret," he told her with a wink. He jerked his thumb at the seat behind him. "That's why I carry a pillow around."

He was kidding. There was no pillow behind him. Liberty felt herself responding to him. There was something incredibly sexy about the detective's wink.

She was fairly certain that if the serial killer had a wink like that, he could undulate incredible waves through his victims.

She couldn't help thinking that all those women, hungry for affection, would easily be susceptible to a wink or attention coming from a smooth, good-looking operator with his own agenda.

So now they had the "how," what they needed was the "why." As in, why was this man killing women and why was he so selective with his victims, targeting only nurses?

Campbell glanced at her again. She had gotten very quiet and that wasn't natural for her, at least not the detective he had gotten to know in the last few days. Something was up.

"Where are you?" Campbell asked.

Clearing his throat, he repeated his question.

Liberty blinked, suddenly aware that he was talking to her.

"Did you say something?" she asked Campbell.

"Yes," he said patiently. "I asked you where you were."

"Lost in a quagmire," she told him.

He frowned at what he felt was a flippant answer. "You need to clear that up for me, Arizona," he told her. "I speak English, I'm fluent in Spanish, and I can manage a little bit of French. I am *not* fluent in gibberish. Sorry."

"I was just thinking that I can't understand how someone who could be so intelligent—like a nurse could just lose all her common sense and go running off like that with someone they really didn't know." Campbell thought he detected a break in her voice as she told him, "Those women's mistake was that they trusted the dating site to live up to its claim they looked into the profiles of all the people appearing on their site."

"There's such a thing as being too trusting," Campbell noted.

"There's also such a thing as being lonely and really hoping against hope that for once in their hard-working life, they had lucked out. You know, like 'other people have happy endings, why not me?' That kind of thing," Liberty pointed out. "It's a terrible thing to be lonely."

He definitely heard something in her voice. He didn't want to pry, but he also didn't want to just back away from the subject she had broached.

"You almost sound as if you're speaking from experience," he told her.

"No," Liberty answered a bit too flatly, dismissing Campbell's suggestion. "But I have a very good imagination and my sympathy gene is alive and well." Then, because he was being concerned and deserved an explanation, she said, "I was looking through my foster mother's things."

That caught his attention. "Are you going to tell me that you discovered your foster mother went on a dating site after all?"

"I honestly don't know," Liberty admitted. "I suppose it might have been a possibility." Staring straight ahead, a sad expression slipped over Liberty's face. "I know she felt she led a good, decent life and wound up accomplishing things, especially in her line of work. She was a great nurse and a fantastic foster mother, but I also know that it wasn't enough to fill the void in her life."

"She talked about that void with you?" Campbell asked, surprised.

She grew silent for a moment then told him, "No, not really. I found her diary almost six months after she had been murdered. The reason I did was because her landlady called me in to clear out her things and get rid of anything I didn't want to keep." A fond smile curved her mouth. "She kept Florence's apartment for as long as she could, but the building owner was putting pressure on Mrs. McGinty to clean up the place and finally get it ready for someone else to rent."

It had been painful, going through all those memories, but she'd managed to force herself to just keep going until it was all packed up.

Campbell didn't understand something. "Isn't it kind of hard to rent out a place where someone was murdered?" he asked.

"But she wasn't killed there," Liberty pointed out. "She was killed while living in the apartment building. There is a difference," she said. "Anyway, I wasn't about to give the landlady a hard time when she was being so nice. I just headed out, packed up Florence's things and never looked back. I did wind up reacquainting myself with what a fantastic, wonderful woman she had been. I mean, I always knew she was a good woman, but she had this huge capacity for caring. I didn't realize at the time how amazing she truly was."

Campbell didn't realize the noise he heard was Liberty quietly crying until he looked at her. At a loss for words, he pulled over to the side of the road and put the gear in Park.

Doing what she could to pull herself together, she scrubbed her hands over her cheeks, getting rid of her telltale tears.

"Why are we stopping?" She wanted to know.

"To give you time to pull yourself together," he told her simply.

Liberty had trouble dealing with his being so thoughtful. "I'm together," she protested, her voice hitching.

"Okay, then to give me a chance to pull myself together," he said cryptically. "Correct me if I'm wrong, but I don't think you ever gave yourself the time to properly grieve."

"There's time enough for grieving when we catch the SOB who did this to her and to all those other women," she said a bit too fiercely.

But he let the vehicle idle. "We're not going anywhere until you get this out of your system."

Her eyes narrowed. "I don't need to get this 'out of my system.'"

"Okay, then *I* need you to get it out of your system. Look, I know how devastated I'd feel in your place. Humor me, Liberty," he told her.

She blinked. "You just called me Liberty," she said in surprise. "Not Arizona."

Campbell shrugged. "Occasionally, I slip," he admitted. "This isn't a nickname moment."

She tried very hard to ignore him, to shrug away his kindness, but she found she just wasn't able to. So when he slipped his arm around her shoulders and drew her closer to him, she struggled to push him away. But then, the next moment, something just broke within her. That was when the tears began to flow in earnest.

"Look what you've done to me," she sobbed.

"Sorry, didn't mean to be understanding, Arizona," he told her.

So, it was back to Arizona, was it? She had to admit that part of her was more comfortable that way. If she was "Arizona," she wasn't being her, which meant she wasn't being vulnerable. She didn't like showing weakness this way.

"Well, you're not forgiven," she informed him.

Then, as he began to give her space, she locked her arms around Campbell and gave in to all the feelings that had suddenly welled up inside her. She just began crying.

Campbell said nothing. He only held her to him and stroked her hair, trying to help her transfer the affection she had felt for Florence to something she was able to handle: the woman's memory.

It helped somewhat.

Chapter 15

Slowly, Liberty felt herself coming around. And on the heels of that came a wave of almost oppressive shame and embarrassment.

Pushing her hair aside and avoiding Campbell's eyes, she did her best to try to pull herself together for the second time that day.

"Sorry, I didn't mean to have such a meltdown," she apologized. Pressing her lips together and venturing a look at Campbell's face, she said, "I know you probably won't believe me, but I don't usually go all to pieces like this."

He gave her a quizzical look. "Why wouldn't I believe you?"

"Because I could just be lying in order to save my pride," Liberty answered.

Campbell shook his head. “Nah, you’re not the type.”

“How would you know?” she questioned. After all, he didn’t really know her.

“Call it instinct,” Campbell answered simply. “I thought I made that clear in the beginning.” He grinned at her. “We Cavanaughs are great believers in gut instincts.”

“You do realize that you make it impossible to argue with you,” she said, blowing out an exasperated breath.

“Good,” he replied, his eyes shining. “That was my plan all along.”

Liberty wasn’t about to take him to task about that. It just sounded too easygoing and nice.

“So where are we off to now?” she asked him, changing the subject.

“To a little town north of here. Gainesville,” he informed her.

“Why Gainesville?” she asked. “What’s in Gainesville?” He hadn’t said anything about it to her earlier.

“Well, thanks to you, I did a little digging and came across a case just like the ones we were looking into. The name didn’t make your original list—the one you brought with you—but the victim was murdered with the exact same MO.”

When did all this happen? They had been together almost constantly since she had arrived. “And when did you do this so-called digging?” Liberty asked.

“Last night, after you went to bed, or at least into the guest room.” He glanced in her direction. Each time he did, he became aware of just how compelling and striking a woman she really was. But he didn't want to make her uncomfortable, so he said, "By the looks of you this morning, you didn't get all that much sleep."

"Flatterer," she quipped dryly, relieved that they were back to bantering and trading barbs. "From the sound of it, you didn't get all that much sleep yourself, either. Why don't you look it?" she asked. The man actually looked rested. That didn't seem fair.

They were on another empty stretch of road and he looked at her for what seemed like a lingering moment. "Because I have the ability to push on like a machine when I need to."

A warm shiver slithered down her back. Why did that sound like a promise to her?

Get a grip, Libby, she lectured herself. *Your recent crying jag must have scrambled your brain.*

"Okay, 'Mr. Machine,'" she said out loud. "How did this 'killing' escape my attention?" She needed to know. "I went through all the reports on strangulation murders that took place in the last four years where the victims were nurses." And then a thought hit her and her eyes widened. "Don't tell me he's gone and broadened his victim base." That would bring them back to square one, she realized, trying not to let that thought bring her down.

Campbell had a different theory about that. "No, but given the timeline, this might be victim zero."

Why would he even think that? Campbell had totally piqued her interest. "Okay, I'm listening. What makes you say that?"

"Well, the exact time that this particular victim—a part-time nurse, by the way—was murdered was a little difficult to pinpoint."

"Why?" Liberty asked. "Was the medical examiner new at the job?" That would have been the simplest explanation, she thought.

"No, the body was buried in the woods. No one found her until after she had been missing for four years," Campbell told her, remembering what he had read. "And then her body was discovered strictly by accident. A construction crew was digging in a newly cleared area to pour the foundation for a building. Ironically enough, the building was intended to be the new police station."

"Business slow?" Liberty quipped. "They had to go digging something up to investigate?"

"Oh, good," Campbell quipped. "You have your sense of humor back."

Liberty was aware of what she had to have sounded like. "Right, if you like your sense of humor on the macabre side."

He looked at her, just relieved that she had managed to lighten up from the way she had been earlier. "Right now, I'll take my humor any way I can get it. We'll work on sides later."

Within another thirty minutes, Campbell had driven to what appeared to be the edge of town.

Liberty scanned the area, rather surprised by what

she saw. The town was the size of an elongated postage stamp. "I didn't think you had towns like this in California. This place is smaller than Calhoun."

"That shouldn't surprise you," he said. "Are you kidding? We have everything in California. You don't have the exclusive rights to tiny towns, Arizona. That is probably part of the reason why this particular murder went unnoticed for as long as it did. I think the residents around here were too stunned to believe that this sort of thing happened in their own town and that there was a monster like this who walked among them."

Liberty agreed completely. "It not an easy thing to come to terms with."

"Let's go talk to Gainesville's police chief and see what he can say to enlighten us about the situation," Campbell told her as he pulled his vehicle up in front of a small, two-story building that called itself the current police station.

"Doesn't look as if they can fit many police officers in here," Campbell commented.

Then he looked in Liberty's direction as they approached the station. Mindful of the fact that she had come from a police station that numbered among its force one chief of police, one detective—her—and two officers, he found himself apologizing, "I'm sorry, was that insensitive?"

"No," she answered. "That's actually rather accurate." Liberty headed toward the station's entrance. "Now let's see if that gut of yours is as fantastic as you claim it is."

Campbell grinned and winked at her. "You're making me blush."

"Oh, right, like that's even remotely possible," she said with a dismissive laugh.

Liberty sincerely doubted if Campbell had *ever* had the ability to blush, not even when he was a kid. But what he did have—and she sincerely appreciated—was the ability to make her feel better. For that—although she wasn't about to tell him—she truly blessed Campbell.

They found the police chief sitting at his desk inside what appeared to be a slightly enlarged cubical of an office. The chief, a giant of a man, was too large for his desk.

Chief Alexander Jenkins III looked up as they walked in and, from his expression, didn't seem surprised to see them. Rising to his feet, he shook first Liberty's hand and then Campbell's.

Liberty caught herself thinking that the man's hands were like big paws, but exceptionally gentle.

"You called ahead?" Liberty asked the detective beside her as he returned the chief's handshake.

"I know my manners. Besides, you can't take a chance on just dropping in without notice. The chief might be out of town on business," he told Liberty between near immobile lips.

Or away cutting down his Christmas tree for the holiday, she thought, which seemed to her to be the more likely scenario.

"Chief Jenkins," Campbell said. "We spoke on the phone earlier this morning. I'm Detective Campbell

Cavanaugh from Aurora and this is Detective Liberty Lawrence from Calhoun, Arizona."

The chief flashed them a wide, welcoming smile. "You people south of us certainly have lyrical names," he observed. Then, with a good-natured shrug, Jenkins told them, "You can call me Al, if you want. My given name is a mouthful," he admitted. The chief gestured to the two chairs standing in front of his desk. "Take a seat. What can I help you with? When we spoke earlier, you said you were working on a serial killer case."

"We are. You said you recently discovered the body of a woman who had gone missing a few years earlier," Campbell prompted.

The chief nodded. "Sarah Hanesworth," he said, supplying them with the victim's name. "We only managed to identify her through her nephew's identification. What do you want to know?"

"Everything," Liberty answered. Without realizing it, she had moved to the edge of her seat. "Did the woman live here?"

"Yes," the chief answered. "The victim moved here a couple of years before she went missing."

"If you don't mind my asking, who reported her missing?" Campbell asked.

"Well, at first no one. That struck me as kind of sad," he confided. "To make no impression on anyone's life so that they don't even realize you're not there anymore. But then the clinic where the victim had worked said she hadn't shown up to work, which struck her boss as rather strange, because she seemed like a conscientious person.

"Since she hadn't been there at the clinic for very long, they considered the fact that maybe she had just taken off to find a better paying position. Then her nephew reported her missing a month later. Said he hadn't heard from her and that he was worried something might have happened to her."

Liberty perked up at the added detail, like a dog spotting a new bone. "And where was he up to this point?" she asked the chief.

"According to the nephew, he was out of town on business. As a matter of fact, to hear him tell it, his business kept him on the road quite a lot. When he swung by, he had only intended on making a quick stop to check in on his aunt, but then her neighbors and the people who worked with her at the clinic said they hadn't seen her, so he got worried and came to me."

The words the chief had used to describe the situation stuck in her mind. "You met him, right?"

"Right."

"Does this nephew strike you as the type who worried?" she asked the chief.

The man's brow furrowed as he tried to understand her question. "Excuse me?"

"Well, you said he was her nephew, and I'm just saying that from my experience, nephews don't generally worry about relatives who they're just occasionally in touch with." For no particular reason, she was experiencing that strange gut feeling again. Something didn't feel right—or maybe it was just her imagination. "Would you have a picture of this concerned nephew?" Liberty asked.

"What are you thinking?" Campbell asked her, interested.

She could only shrug and admit, "I don't know yet."

"Fair enough," Campbell said agreeably. "I'm sure there must be a picture of the guy somewhere. Since he's on the road so much, at the very least, he's got to have a driver's license."

"Hanesworth," Liberty said, repeating the family's last name. "Can't be that hard to locate."

But the chief shot her down by shaking his head. "Her nephew had a different last name than she did."

"Why am I not surprised?" Liberty murmured.

"All right, then what *is* this nephew's last name?" Campbell asked.

"Give me a second," the chief requested as he began to flip through the papers inside the report. "It's here in the report," Jenkins said. "He was the one who identified the victim's body." Finding what he was looking for, he skimmed down the page—and then frowned. "Well, that doesn't ring a bell."

That didn't sound good, Liberty thought. "What doesn't?"

"The nephew's name." He looked up from the report. "I'm sure that's not what he told me, or what I thought I wrote in the report." And then he shrugged. "But I guess it must have been. It's right here." The chief tapped the page where he had found the information. "I guess I must have had a memory lapse."

Campbell was still chewing on the manner. "You said that this nephew was out on the road a lot."

"Yes?" the chief asked.

Campbell was playing a hunch. For the moment, what he was considering provided one possible explanation. "What does he do that takes him on the road? Is he a salesman?" the detective asked.

"No, he said that he services and updates those new computers. Tried to talk me into one, but I wouldn't have any part of it," he admitted rather proudly.

"Fixes them? Programs them? Or...?" Campbell questioned, letting his voice trail off and leaving it for the chief to provide a suitable answer.

"I'm afraid your guess is as good as mine," Jenkins confessed. "You do know that this is officially a cold case, right?"

"Doesn't mean it can't heat up," Campbell told him. "And as for what Sarah Hanesworth's nephew does for a living, my guess is that it gives him the ability to alter whatever was originally input on a computer."

The light bulb went off over the chief's head. "Like his name?" the chief asked.

"Like his name," Campbell agreed.

"Wow," the chief murmured, clearly floored by the theory.

"That would be my word for it," Liberty agreed. "You said the victim and her nephew moved here a couple of years before she went missing?"

"That's right." The chief waited for another question to follow.

He didn't have long to wait.

"Would you happen to know where they originally came from?" she asked.

"Well, his file appears to be rather creatively worked on," the chief said with more than a note of skepticism in his voice.

"All right, what about hers?" Campbell asked. "She had to have filled out an employment form or something to that effect when she initially applied for her job."

Campbell had a feeling that they were being too optimistic in their projection. "Little towns like this have a tendency—at times—to resist change, to cling to the old way things were done rather than go with the innovative."

In which case, he thought, the sort of information they were looking to gain access to might not be available.

But the chief proudly shook his head. "Well, not me. I enjoy progress and everything that it might bring with it."

"Then hopefully, there are other people in town who think the same way you do and we'll be able to find a rather decent picture of Sarah's nephew to work with," Liberty said.

She wanted the photograph so badly, she could almost taste it.

"Then I guess I'd best get started on that." Getting up and heading to the doorway, the chief called out, "Hey, Abe. I've got an assignment for you. And bring your glasses." He glanced over his shoulder at the two detectives behind him. "He's always leaving them on his desk. Insists that he doesn't need them," the chief confided, lowering his voice, "but between you and me, he really does."

The officer who responded to the chief's summons looked utterly unenthusiastic as he ambled into the office. "Can't this keep?" he asked. "I was just about to take off, Chief."

"If you don't mind, I'd like you to delay that take-off, Abe," the chief requested, his tone leaving no space for an argument. "I've got a little hunting assignment for you."

The young police officer's face lit up at the mere mention of the word *hunting*.

"Sir? What do you want me to go hunting for?" he asked eagerly. It was obvious that he enjoyed hunting.

"I want you to find a photograph of Sarah Hanesworth's nephew. You know, the guy who came in to identify her after they found her buried where they were planning on pouring the foundation for the new police building—the one they currently have on hold," the chief added for Campbell and Liberty's benefit.

"Oh." Abe's face fell at least half a foot. His disappointed was almost palatable.

Chapter 16

Frowning, the chief watched his police officer dejectedly lumber out of the room to an adjacent area.

"As you can see by Abe's face, I'm not sure just how long it's going to take to locate a picture of this guy you're asking about. We're a small town, but we're not *that* small. Ideally, we should have it at our fingertips but, well…" The chief's voice trailed off as he rubbed the fingertips of his right hand together, signifying that what they were looking for might have very well just slipped through the cracks.

"So, the way I see it," he continued, addressing the two visiting police detectives, "you have one of two ways to go. You can either drive back down to Aurora and return tomorrow, or we've got a couple of nice family hotels where you can rent rooms for the night. I can personally vouch that the food is good and the bedding is clean at least in one of them. I've had to stay there on one occasion."

The chief had aroused Campbell's curiosity. "If you don't mind my asking, why would you have to stay in a hotel in a town where you live?"

"I don't mind. That was the unfortunate result of having one of my kids leave the front door open and a skunk deciding to wander in. Our dog, Scout, took offense and started to raise a storm, defending us. Needless to say, he didn't fare very well." The chief shook his head as he recalled the incident. "The poor guy stank up the whole house. The upshot was that we wound up going to the hotel while our place was aired out."

Liberty knew that most hotels didn't welcome pets, especially not ones that smelled like a skunk. Concerned about what had happened to the poor pet, she asked, "Where did the dog stay?"

Obviously getting her drift, the chief smiled as he answered her. "We have a very understanding vet who boarded Scout for us. Doc Adams worked hard and finally managed to get that awful smell to dissipate.

"Anyway," he said, resuming his story, "those are your choices. Aurora or one of the local hotels. So what'll it be?"

Campbell glanced in Liberty's direction and said, "We'll go back to Aurora. It's not *that* far and I sleep better in my own bed," he confessed.

The nature of his response surprised her, but Liberty decided to make no comment.

"Thanks for all your help, Chief," Campbell went on. "We'll get out of your hair now and, if everything goes well, we'll be back to see you in the morning."

The chief nodded, glancing in his officer's direction. "Hopefully, Abe over there can make heads or tails out of all the paperwork he's wading through," the chief said as he walked his two visitors to the front door of the police station.

Liberty merely smiled at the man as they parted company but said nothing. Instead, she waited until she and Campbell were back in the latter's vehicle and were driving toward Aurora before she asked, "Why did you say that?"

The question, coming completely out of the blue the way it did, totally threw him. He had no idea what she was referring to.

"Say what?" Campbell asked.

It was dark now and since he was in an unfamiliar area, he decided it wouldn't hurt to have a little extra insurance. He hit the GPS navigating system, pressing Home to help guide him on the unfamiliar road.

He knew damn well what she was talking about, Liberty thought. "That you have trouble sleeping in anything but your own bed. Weren't you the one who told me that you could fall asleep hanging on a hook in the closet? What you said to the chief about not being able to sleep in a strange bed was for my benefit, wasn't it?"

"I have no idea what you're talking about," Campbell told her innocently.

Okay, she thought. She'd play along and spell it out

for him. "You didn't want me having to admit that I have trouble sleeping in strange places. You probably thought admitting to something personal like that would make me uncomfortable," she guessed. Liberty shifted in her seat and stared at his profile. "You really are gallant, aren't you?"

She was torn between thinking that he was too good to be true and thinking that, for some reason, Campbell was just playing her due to some hidden agenda of his own design.

Instead of giving her a teasing answer the way she would have expected, Campbell told her, "I was always taught never to make anyone uncomfortable if I could possibly help it—unless, of course, they were the scum of the earth." He glanced at her as he flashed his thousand-watt smile in her direction. "And you, Arizona, definitely do not qualify for that description."

He fell silent for a moment, as if thinking, before looking back at the road. "Look, it's going to be at least another half hour, if not more, before we get back home, so if you want to sack out and take a catnap, I'm okay with that."

He was saying that he absolved her of her obligation of staying awake and keeping him company with mindless conversation. Well, she could hold up her end as well as he could.

"I don't take catnaps or any other sort of furry animal naps. I'm fine," Liberty informed him in no uncertain terms.

The way she saw it, since he had to stay awake,

the least she could do was remain awake with him and provide moral support—or take over driving altogether—if for some reason the mighty "superhero" began to suddenly fade on her.

Campbell shrugged at her protest. "Have it your way, Arizona. I was just trying to be thoughtful."

She made what sounded like a dismissive sound under her breath. "Don't overdo it."

Because the road had straightened somewhat, he felt he could risk sparing her another, longer glance.

"Wow, it's like trying to walk a tightrope with you," he marveled. "One wrong step and it's all over." He shook his head at what that seemed to convey. "You might want to rethink that approach."

Liberty felt a stab of guilt. Did she really come across as being that difficult? she couldn't help wondering. She certainly hadn't meant to.

She was about to attempt to make some sort of an apology to Campbell when he suddenly changed the subject on her. She had a feeling he was doing it to spare her again.

"So tell me about this gut feeling you have concerning the case we're working." He asked her, "What's up with that?"

She didn't want to make it seem as if she were making a big deal out of it. Having been the object of ridicule more than once, for more reasons than one, she had become very careful about not setting herself up.

"I could be all wrong," she prefaced, wanting him to be aware that *she* was aware of that.

"That's already been taken into consideration," Campbell told her. "But I saw that expression on your face when those wheels in your head started turning, Arizona." That in turn coaxed another memory to the foreground and he laughed. "If I didn't know any better, I'd say that you almost qualify to be an honorary Cavanaugh. I've seen that same look on my brothers' faces, not to mention on the faces of a number of other relatives."

Campbell was staring straight ahead at an almost hypnotic road as he navigated them toward home. He was trying his best to distract himself. "Tell me what you're thinking—without the disclaimers," he warned, aware now of how she tended to work.

She was still a little hesitant to share this outright. "Well, it might be just a coincidence—"

"But?" he asked when her voice stopped. "And remember, I said no disclaimers."

"Right," Liberty nodded as she forged ahead. "Don't you think that it's rather odd that first this computer-expert nephew *doesn't* worry when he can't get in touch with his aunt—the aunt who brought him with her when she moved. And then he files a missing person's report after waiting more than a month after this woman who supposedly raised him and put a roof over his head had disappeared?"

He thought of possible explanations and the most common one came to mind.

"Well, a lot of pseudo-adult kids and their parents, especially substitute parents, don't stay close or even see eye to eye. There could even be a period of estrangement before things eventually smooth themselves out."

"Is your family like that?" she asked.

"Actually," he admitted, "I guess you could say that my family is the exception to the rule. And as for this MIA nephew, maybe he was just busy and assumed everything was fine with his aunt. That's another way to go."

"Maybe." Liberty seemed to almost chew on the word before it finally emerged.

Campbell spared her another look. The road had become better lit in this latest section so he didn't feel he was flirting with a possible accident if he looked away for a split second.

"But your gut tells you no," he guessed from the tone of her voice.

Liberty sighed, feeling as if she were opening herself up for possible ridicule. But he did ask. "My gut has a mind of its own."

Rather than laugh at her, he seemed almost delighted. "Oh, Uncle Brian is going to love you." Campbell guaranteed.

She'd heard him mention the name before.

"Which one is he again?" she asked.

There were just too many names to remember that weren't case-related. She had no trouble remembering all the names of the thirty—now thirty-two—serial killer victims, but when it came to the large volume of her temporary partner's family members, she had to admit it was somewhat confusing.

"He's the Chief of D's," Campbell patiently reminded her.

"Right," Liberty responded, sounding for all the world as if she was humoring him.

"Do you guys wear name tags, you know, when you get together or do you just avoid using any proper names at all to avoid calling someone by the wrong one?" she asked him.

"That generally doesn't happen," he told her. "Newcomers to the family ranks make mistakes at times, but no one minds. We're aware of how overwhelming the ranks might be at first sight." And then he smiled broadly. "And you'll get to find out yourself soon enough."

That put her instantly on the alert. "What do you mean by that?"

"Well, if I know Uncle Andrew, and I do—" he emphasized with a grin "—he's about due to have one of his 'family gatherings' and your being here has provided him with the perfect excuse to throw one—not to mention that it's almost Christmas and that's when he has his biggest blowout. This year Uncle Andrew probably feels that he has double the excuse to have one of those big gatherings."

This didn't sound real to Liberty, especially considering her emotionally impoverished background. It was something she wouldn't have even dreamed about.

"You're kidding, right?" she asked Campbell.

He congratulated himself on maintaining a straight

face as he told her, "Parties are very serious business to Uncle Andrew."

She was having trouble wrapping her head around that. It was hard to believe that these people were actually real. And yet, that same gut that had her attempting to unscramble the clues to finding this serial killer told her that the Cavanaughs were all very real.

The words just slipped out before she could think to censor herself. "I would have given my eyeteeth to have been placed with a family like yours when I was growing up," she said wistfully.

Liberty pressed her lips together as she shut her eyes. *Terrific, you've probably just scared the man.*

And then she heard him say, "Well, it's never too late to rectify things." Campbell sounded almost too serious.

Liberty felt her cheeks redden and blessed the darkness that hid that from Campbell.

She resorted to humor in an attempt to distract the detective from her discomfort over opening herself up to this extent.

"Right," she wisecracked, "your family's going to adopt me."

Rather than laugh at the idea, or say anything flippant that would result in putting the whole thing to bed, Campbell told her, "Why don't we just take this thing one step at a time, Arizona, and see where it winds up going?"

Stunned, she just looked at him for a long moment. "You are the strangest man," she marveled.

"I've been called more flattering things in my time, but I'll accept it," he told Liberty.

Feeling somewhat awkward, she focused on her surroundings and was relieved to see some signs that were beginning to look somewhat familiar to her.

Looks like we're home, Toto, she thought, watching the road. "I think we just crossed into the city limits," she said to Campbell.

He laughed, knowing full well what she was really saying. "And just in time, too, right?"

Liberty didn't attempt to deny it. "You said it, I didn't."

"Just putting your thoughts into words," he told her. Within minutes, he was pulling into the residential area where his garden apartment was located. And then into his carport.

"No," she corrected him, referring to his previous explanation. "You're putting words *into* my mouth and I am very capable of speaking for myself."

Amen to that, Campbell mused silently. "No argument there."

Getting out, Campbell circled around the back of his vehicle and went to open the door on her side. But Liberty had already opened it.

He put his hand out to help guide her, then withdrew it when she gained her feet. This one, he thought, was independent to a fault.

"All right, what shall we argue about now?" Campbell asked her as he led the way to the stairway to his second-floor apartment.

Liberty didn't understand why he would say that.

"What makes you think that we're going to argue?" she asked.

To her way of thinking, they had just spent a long, exhausting, but very productive day, and that fact went a very long way to making her happy, not argumentative.

His eyes met hers. "History repeating itself," he answered.

"Well, think again," she told him, waiting for him to open the door.

The key slid out of his hand, falling to the cheerful but slightly dusty doormat that welcomed everyone to a Happy Home.

Campbell made the mistake of bending to retrieve the key at the very same moment that Liberty did the very same thing.

The result was predictable: they bumped heads and stumbled backward.

His hand flying to his forehead, Campbell reached out to grab Liberty's hand with the other in an attempt to steady her. He barely succeeded.

"We couldn't have played that any better than if we were following the actual script for a skit," he said.

Liberty winced as she attempted to right herself as she rose to her feet.

"Except, in a skit," she told him, "I have a feeling that my head wouldn't feel like it just played the part of a cracked egg." Belatedly, she looked at Campbell, concerned. "Does yours hurt?"

"Not so much." He grinned. "But if I was a kid and

this happened, this would be the part that I would ask you to kiss the boo-boo."

She blinked, staring at him. "I'm sorry?"

"Nothing to be sorry about," he assured her. "You were just trying to be polite and pick up my keys. What happened was an accident. I absolve you," Campbell told her lightly.

"Still, that doesn't negate the hurt you sustained when we crashed into one another."

He paused to smile at her. "Having you around negates the hurt."

Liberty stared at him, confused. "What is that supposed to even mean?"

"Anything you want it to." With that, he unlocked his front door. Holding the door open, he let her enter first.

When she did, she took exactly three steps and stopped dead.

The apartment had *not* looked like this when they had left this morning. "Um, Cavanaugh, don't look now, but I think someone broke into your place and decorated it." When she turned around to look at him, she was surprised to see that he *wasn't* surprised.

And with good reason.

"That would probably be the work of one of my sisters. Maybe both. Jacqui and Blythe are both off this week and they knew I was busy working on this case with you."

She was doing her best to understand the logic. "So they broke in and decorated?"

He laughed at her question. "Pretty much."

Well, she reasoned, *they probably have the resources for it*. “You were all probably born with silver spoons in your mouths.”

“No,” he denied, “but with a strong work ethic and an even stronger sense of family. Now this talk is tabled for the night. You need to get to bed.”

His unexpected declaration had her heart beginning to hammer.

Hard.

Why did those incredibly simple words sound like an invitation to her?

And why in the world did she desperately want it to be?

Chapter 17

Looking back, what happened in the moments after that almost seemed as if it was just all a blur. Liberty really wasn't sure exactly how any of it transpired, only that, deep down, she was incredibly happy that it had.

Maybe it was even spurred on by the possibility that they were finally getting somewhere with this soul-sucking case that had all but pushed her over the brink.

Or maybe what ultimately transpired just happened because she was tired and, as such, was far from being able to think clearly.

Although, when she reflected on it later, a better explanation was that Campbell's kind, understanding manner had opened something within her that made her capable of *feeling* something beyond a sense of duty for the very first time in her life.

Not to mention the fact that what she was experiencing had somehow taken down the protective barriers she had always *always* kept up around her heart.

For whatever the reason, whatever the cause, all Liberty really knew was that one moment Campbell was leaving her at the guest room door, telling her to get some well-earned rest, and the very next moment, she was calling out his name.

Campbell turned from the doorway and looked at her.

"Did you want something?"

He asked the question so quietly, Liberty could barely hear him. Quite honestly, she almost *felt* him say the words rather than heard him say them.

She whispered her response in the same tone.

"Yes."

The single word seemed to come on its own accord, propelled by an inner desire that—again—she had been totally unaware of feeling but that had somehow bloomed, full-bodied, within her, taking up every inch of space she had to offer.

What it came down to was a matter of their souls communicating without an actual exchange of words.

The look in her eyes when she raised them to his face was what ultimately pulled Campbell in.

Moreover, it was that very same look within her expressive eyes that had him putting his arms around Liberty and pulling her to him.

Campbell had always been a great believer in the

fact that there were times when actions really did speak louder than words. And this, he thought, was obviously that time for him.

His eyes holding hers captive, Campbell leaned forward and let his lips silently do his talking for him.

He kissed her with such force, such emotion, the very act almost completely undid her.

Liberty not only found herself responding to his kiss, but hungering for more. She didn't even remember putting her arms around his neck, they were just suddenly there. It was as much to hold herself steady as to press her body against his.

There were no words to express how much she enjoyed that.

His warmth filled her.

Stirred her.

Made her head feel as if it were spinning almost dangerously out of control.

Liberty's arms tightened around the back of his neck and the pressure of her mouth increased. And as it did, the very act ignited them both.

It was as if this one single action—kissing her with total abandonment—opened the door to all the rest, giving him permission to do what his soul was begging him to do: worship her with his hands, with his mouth, with the fingertips that were lovingly caressing all the tempting, supple curves she had to offer.

Because of how dedicated he had inadvertently become to the career path he had chosen, Campbell was fairly certain the simple happiness that could be found within the life other members of his family had been fortunate enough to all but stumble across would wind up eluding him.

Not for any concrete, hard and fast reason he could actually point to or cite, but because there were only so many hours in the day and his hours were taken up by his work.

And then this woman had all but dropped into his life from out of practically nowhere.

It was almost as if it was fate. This woman with her doe eyes and her utterly overwhelming vulnerability had him suddenly feeling things he had only enviously heard about from other family members.

Like feeling the desire to protect her, to make her happiness one of his main priorities.

This was what it meant to be more than just mildly attracted to a woman, Campbell thought.

He felt his excitement building. He couldn't wait to discover what else this interlude would reveal to him about this woman and this wondrous experience he found himself on the brink of.

The passion was all but exploding within him, but Campbell forced himself to move slowly, like a man working his way across a very thin tightrope stretched across a raging river.

He didn't want to rush this first experience between them, no matter how very urgent his own needs felt.

Most of all, Campbell didn't want to take a chance on frightening Liberty off—just in case she misunderstood his intentions.

In truth, there was nothing holding him back—

except a lifetime of common sense and his own family values to serve as a yardstick.

But good intentions or not, restraining himself certainly wasn't easy.

Not when he really wanted to rip away her clothes, and especially not when he felt her hands slipping in under his shirt, loosening the belt buckle on his trousers and then almost seductively tugging the material away from his hips.

He saw the desire and need growing in her eyes, mirroring that same desire and need echoing in his soul, Campbell realized, his breath catching in his throat.

"If I didn't know any better, I'd say you were looking to have your way with me," Campbell breathed, pressing a small network of light kisses along her face and down her neck.

"Then you'd be right," she answered in a voice so very low it all but rippled along his skin to register.

The fact that Campbell's breathing was audible and growing more so had the totally unexpected side benefit of turning Liberty on to an overwhelming degree. The very sound of his breathing caused her heart to hammer so wildly, she was certain it was just about to break through her chest.

And it seemed even more inclined to do so as she felt his hands touching her—slowly—in all the important, very sensitive places.

Touching her.

Possessing her.

Making her permanently and indelibly his as he undressed her.

Liberty would have died before ever letting him suspect this, but she had gone past the point of no return.

If she had been able to think about it, Liberty really couldn't remember the last time she had been intimate with a man—or the last time she had even wanted to be.

But this…this was something else again. Something so intense, it brought her reaction to an entirely new level. She felt as if she were running toward a goal. A goal that involved submerging herself in unending waves of ecstasy as she lay beneath him on the bed.

Rather than finding himself satiated, with every passing moment, every passing warm, hot kiss, Campbell just wanted more.

More of this wondrous sensation.

More of her.

And unless she suddenly decided to abruptly put a stop to things, he intended to continue with this incredible journey until they were both just spent puffs of smoke.

Liberty had turned out to be an endless source of wonder for him and he was dying to find out if this experience would ultimately live up to all his expectations.

Because it certainly felt that way.

When Campbell realized that he couldn't hold out

any longer, he slowly and completely anointed her with his mouth and tongue one last time.

And then he slid his primed and ready body up along hers.

One look into her eyes told him that Liberty was more than ready for him. Kissing her deeply and thereby intensifying the union that was to be, he gently entered her.

Holding her, pressing his body against hers, Campbell began to move.

At first he moved slowly, then with mounting intensity, going faster and faster until they were both caught up in this heated carnal marathon, breathlessly racing to the very pinnacle of the mountain and that delicious, final, mind-blowing explosive moment.

When it happened, enveloping and ensnaring them both in an incredibly gratifying euphoria, Campbell and Liberty fell back against the bed. They were desperately trying to catch their breath and to remember exactly where they were within this wild, mazelike new place they had just stumbled across and discovered.

Like victims of a mass hypnosis, their brains felt completely disoriented.

"Are you all right?" Campbell asked the woman lying in the crook of his arm when he finally felt he could speak without having his voice just disappear.

"I'm not sure," Liberty admitted. "What just happened here?"

His smile was soft and just a little stunned. "I think we just might have crossed over to another world, Arizona." His arm tucked around her, he drew Liberty a shade closer to his side. "You are really a revelation, you know. I had a feeling that you had a more smoldering side beneath all that civilized calm, but *this* was way beyond anything I could have possibly imagined."

"Good imagined?" she asked almost shyly even though she was desperately attempting to project an air of nonchalance.

"'Good' doesn't even begin to describe it," Campbell told her honestly. "As a matter of fact, I don't think a word has been invented to begin to describe the magnitude of what just occurred here in this small, heretofore peaceful bedroom."

"Peaceful, right." She laughed at his description. "Like before this evening, you were living the life of a monk."

"Not a monk exactly," Campbell allowed, pressing a kiss to her forehead. "But definitely not at that escalated level I found myself visiting with you just minutes earlier," he told her.

Before she could stop, she heard herself telling him, "I really wish I could believe you."

He crooked his finger beneath her chin and brought her head up so that she could meet his eyes.

"You can," he told her in all seriousness.

Damn it, but she found herself believing him. She knew that would be a mistake of the first order. But she believed him because she really *wanted* to believe him.

That would be a super mistake, Liberty reminded

herself. One she was too smart to allow herself to make. For one thing, it would negate all the residual, wonderful benefits of what had just gone down between them.

This was not about laying the groundwork for the future, this was just an exquisite interlude she had had the very excellent good fortune to have experienced.

That should be enough.

Liberty tried to deflect the effect his words had on her. But it wasn't easy.

"I guess that's what makes you such a good detective," she told him. "You have this way about you that gets people to believe what you're telling them. It's a rare gift."

He surprised her by not arguing the point but by agreeing with her. "It is." He nodded, slowly stroking her skin in small, sensual circles. "And I do have it. But you're not 'people,'" he told her.

She didn't understand where he was going with this. "I'm not?"

"You're not. You, Arizona, are in a category all by yourself," he told her.

She sighed, flattered in her own way although not yet ready to be taken in by what he was saying. She was also too tired to argue with him about this, so she let it stand.

"Okay, I give up," Liberty told him. "Have it your way."

His eyes shone. "Thanks. With your permission, I fully intend to."

Liberty could have sworn that she was officially

being put on notice, but then, she thought, that wasn't really such a bad thing, was it?

She shifted her body into his. "I guess, then, we had better get started before it gets to be 'tomorrow,'" she told him.

He was already nibbling on her lips. "That…is… an…excel…lent…idea."

Before she could lace her arms around his neck and curl up against the man who had woken all these new and deliciously tantalizing feelings within her body, the cell phone Campbell had in the pocket of his trousers began to ring.

"Leave it. It's probably a nuisance call," she guessed. But even as she said it, she knew neither one of them would be able to just ignore it. Not picking up wasn't acceptable.

"Probably," he agreed, reaching for the cell, which was now a resident of the bedroom floor. "But just in case, we did hand out both our numbers today. Maybe someone remembered something."

"Or wants to sell us on a new medical breakthrough," Liberty said, which was more likely the case.

Finding the phone, he got back into bed as he pressed in his password. "*You* are enough of a medical breakthrough for me," Campbell assured her. "Cavanaugh here," he said into his cell.

It took listening to the person on the other end say several words before Campbell realized that the chief from up north was calling him. The name coming in on his screen had gotten somehow garbled.

"Well, it took him half the night, but he did it," the

chief almost crowed. "Abe found the information on that dead woman's nephew."

Liberty watched the detective suddenly sit up very straight, as if good posture made the news all the more important. "We'll be right up there," Campbell promised.

"I'll be waiting for you at the police station," she could hear the chief's voice promise.

Liberty was already throwing off the sheets on her side of the bed.

Chapter 18

Campbell quickly hurried into the clothes that had been discarded on the floor earlier when he and Liberty had made love.

"That was the chief," he told Liberty.

"I gathered that much," she answered as she hustled into her own clothing.

Apparently the pullover top she had worn earlier had somehow managed to find its way into a knot. Muttering under her breath, she did her best to undo it so she could just pull it on.

As he finished getting dressed, Campbell continued to talk and fill her in. "That officer working for him managed to find that woman's nephew."

She wondered how sleepy Campbell thought she

was that she would have missed that. "Yes, I gathered that, too," she told him as she zipped up her jeans.

Her shoes had somehow found their way across the room, although she couldn't remember kicking them off. Liberty grabbed them up and made her way back to the bed to slip the shoes on.

Finished, Campbell turned to look at her. He was surprised to find that Liberty was already dressed as well.

"Look, I can take it from here," he told her. The statement managed to surprise her. "You don't have to come if you're exhausted."

Liberty blinked. She couldn't have been more stunned than if Campbell had just declared that he really thought that the world was flat.

"Hold on. Back up," she ordered, raising her hand like a traffic cop. "I'm not any more exhausted than you are—and besides, we're going to be driving there. I'm not going to be flapping my wings and flying there," she pointed out. "So unless there's another reason you don't want me coming along—and it had better be a damn good one—I'm coming."

Campbell raised his hands high in exaggerated surrender. He should have known she would react that way. "I'm just trying to be thoughtful, Arizona," he told her.

She allowed herself brief contact and brushed her hand against his cheek. "You took care of that little detail earlier," she said very seriously. "Okay, let's go," she declared, heading for the door.

Following her, Campbell felt obligated to tell her,

"You know, you do look like an unmade bed." He punctuated his statement with a laugh.

"Maybe," she allowed. "But I *am* ready."

Within minutes, they were back in Campbell's vehicle and on the road heading toward the town they had left behind them less than four hours ago.

A lifetime ago, Liberty couldn't help thinking, given what had happened between them since they had left Gainesville.

"When he called, did the chief say anything else about this nephew?" she asked.

"Only that there might have been a slight glitch in the file," Campbell told her, choosing his words very carefully.

"What sort of a glitch?" she asked suspiciously, attempting to brace herself for who knew what.

"Turns out the nephew isn't a traveling IT guy after all," Campbell told her.

That managed to catch her by surprise. "Then what is he?"

Campbell slanted a glance in her direction, confident that this would undoubtedly knock her for a loop. "Well, according to what was just uncovered, the nephew just might be an FBI informant."

She blinked, certain that she had misheard him or her brain was playing tricks on her, stealing her ability to concentrate. Maybe Campbell was right. Maybe she was too tired to come along on this trip.

Still she asked, "Say what?"

"An FBI informant," Campbell repeated, enunciating the words very slowly.

Liberty felt her jaw drop. She was about to tell him that was someone's idea of a macabre joke, or an absurd fabrication, when the direct opposite hit her and she considered the idea.

"You know, that just might make sense," she said. Her face became animated as she straightened. She could see that he was about to discount the theory. She started talking quickly. "Think about it. He's tracking nurses, professional women. He has to come across as someone in their league. Working with the FBI puts him in that rarefied capacity. *And* if he just happened to have enough computer tech savvy to be able to hack into those dating sites, maybe he's looking for a certain type, which would require him unearthing some pertinent background information." She was all but tripping over her own tongue to get this all out. "Well, he's got that covered, too."

Liberty glanced at the speedometer on the dashboard. "Can you drive this thing any faster?"

"Not safely," Campbell pointed out. Because the road they were on was empty, they were already exceeding the allowable speed limit. To go any faster would really be pushing it. "Besides, what's the hurry? It's not like we're going to catch this guy leisurely sauntering through town."

"I know that," she answered impatiently, "but once we have his file and the additional information, we'll be one step closer to bringing this guy down."

Campbell made no comment but he grinned broadly in her direction.

"What's so funny?" she asked. It was dark, but

she could detect his smile by the curve of his cheek. He had a nice smile, but she didn't want it being at her expense.

"There really *is* an optimist inside you," Campbell happily declared.

"You ought to know," she told him, thinking of the wonderful interlude they had just spent together. "You put her there."

That brought an even heartier laugh from him. "You can thank me for that once we're back in bed again."

She thought of everything that stretched ahead of them before they could get back. "That might not happen for a long time."

"Maybe not," he agreed, nodding. "But it is something for us to hold on to."

Lord help her, but he did make her feel special. Or at the very least, Liberty thought, that they had some sort of a small future ahead. Nothing major—she wasn't expecting to be lucky enough for what had happened between them to turn into a permanent thing. But from the sound of things, it might survive the weekend—and maybe a tiny bit beyond that point.

Don't do it, Lib. Don't count those chickens before the hen even gets to lay those eggs. Remember the Merriweathers, she cautioned herself.

The Merriweathers had been the closest thing to a perfect family she had encountered in her young life, and they had seemed interested in taking her in. The key word here being *seemed.* In the end, they had gone with a blond-haired, blue-eyed girl named

Mandy who looked as if she had been created expressly with the Merriweathers in mind. It was almost as if she'd been literally *designed* to fit into their Christmas photographs.

And Liberty…well, she had been too skinny, her hair too straggly looking.

At that point, Liberty had completely given up any and all hope of finding a family to belong to and just decided to go her own way—until Florence had unexpectedly come into her life.

The thought of Florence had Liberty freshly resolving to find this so-called nephew—or whatever he was—and pump him to within an inch of his life. If the creep turned out to be the serial killer, she'd know it, she promised herself. And if he turned out *not* to be the killer, she was certain that she would know that, too.

Campbell glanced at her. Liberty had become far quieter than he was accustomed to her being.

"Everything okay?" he asked.

"No, but I have every faith that it's going to be," Liberty told him with what seemed like unshakable conviction.

He knew that she had nothing else to base it on except for a feeling. But, hell, he was a Cavanaugh, so that "gut" feeling was definitely good enough for him.

Dawn was beginning to just stir the brilliant colors on the horizon when they finally pulled into town.

There was no sign of traffic—or life, for that matter—in the streets. Gainesville was one of those towns that made her think of the phrase "rolled up the sidewalks at night." This town certainly had rolled up theirs, but now, here and there, there were signs of people waking up.

"There's a light in the police station," she pointed out eagerly.

"I see it," he answered, dispensing with the urge to comment that at least they didn't do their work in the dark.

"Sorry," she apologized, knowing she was allowing her enthusiasm to get the best of her. "I didn't mean to suggest that you didn't."

"That's okay, I forgive you," he told her with a wink. "Let's go see what the chief has to show us."

Campbell was aware that Chief Jenkins could have forwarded the information he had acquired, but knew it would be better received if Liberty could actually hold the file in her hands. That way, she would also be able to ask the chief any pertinent questions.

Getting out of the vehicle, they walked into the station.

They found the chief in, but he had his arms crossed in front of him on his desk and was resting his head on the semicircle they had formed. The man had obviously spent the night in the office combing through all the information they had asked for.

"Nice to know that there are dedicated men even out here in the sticks," Campbell said to Liberty in a hushed voice.

"Hey, watch it with that 'sticks' comment. As for me, I wouldn't expect anything else from the law officers working in a small town," Liberty told him in all seriousness.

She abruptly stopped speaking as she saw the chief stirring. The man emitted a little moan as he moved his stiff shoulders.

"I can hear you, you know. I wasn't sleeping," the chief told her. "I was just resting my eyes."

Campbell was not about to argue with the man. "As well you should be, given that you've been working around the clock to help us find that woman's nephew, not to mention getting us that much closer to the serial killer we're looking to bring down."

The chief flashed him a smile, knowing full well that the detective was padding the scenario. "You've got a good way of putting things," he told Campbell. "You ever get tired of working in Aurora, I can always find a place for you here."

Rather than politely turn him down, or tell the chief about the huge network of family members working in the city he was from, Campbell politely thanked the chief for his offer. "Thanks. I'll be sure to keep that in mind." Out of the corner of his eye, he could see that Liberty was all but biting her tongue not to interrupt and ask a whole barrage of questions.

"So," he began, doing his best to keep this all as low-key as possible, "just what did your police officer find?"

"Well, from all indications, this nephew is either a very busy, very clever guy who works with computers as well as that secret life that's been hinted at in the records—or the man really knows how to lie—

big-time." The chief looked at the two people in his office. "The final verdict is up in the air. Anyone want to hazard a guess?" the chief asked.

"Maybe it's a little bit of both. Or he's exaggerating so much just to put us off," Liberty told the two men.

"Come again?" Campbell asked.

"Think about it. He laid it on so thickly in this file because it's true, but he was trying to throw off whoever was reading the file by making it sound as if it couldn't possibly be true, that he couldn't be accomplishing as much as he claimed he did, juggling two lives. And thereby making that so-called double life of his that much easier to lead.

"You know, it's more of a case of 'now you see him, now you don't.' Except in this case, you don't know exactly who it is you're seeing," she concluded, looking from one man to the other to see if they agreed with her.

The two men looked a little puzzled for a moment, and then Campbell nodded at her. "You know, in a strange, lopsided way of thinking, that actually makes some sort if sense."

"Of course it does," Liberty answered. It was actually very simple. There was one main thought at the root of all this.

"Serial killers think they're smarter than everyone else, and that, sooner or later, leads to their downfall. We just have to hope that it's sooner than later. Now is this his real name, or is he using an alias?" She wanted to know, pointing to a line in the folder.

"Better yet, give me any names that you have on file for this guy."

She turned hopefully toward Campbell. "Can Valri do a deep dive into all the available records to see just how much information there is available on this so-called 'broken up' nephew who keeps pulling these disappearing acts?"

"Valri?" the chief questioned, looking from Liberty to the detective with her.

Liberty had gotten so caught up in the file, she had almost forgotten that the chief was there. "Valri Cavanaugh is one of his cousins," she explained, nodding at Campbell.

"Valri is a total computer wizard. If it can be found on the internet, or even somewhere on the dark web, Valri is the one who can find it."

"Can she now?" the chief asked, impressed. "She sounds like a really good person to know, especially since our own officer, Abe, doubles as a computer tech, but his computer skills leave something to be desired," the chief told them.

Liberty felt a little guilty, flaunting Valri's abilities in front of the chief. "I have to tell you that she's pretty pressed for time from morning to night. Most of the time, she gets things done but only by working an inordinate amount of hours," she said, quoting what Campbell had told her. "The poor woman hardly has a private life outside the office."

"Well, other than this guy—" the chief nodded at the file on the desk "—we don't really have anything that would even begin to interest your computer wizard. No need to worry," he assured them. "I won't be calling her. Here." He pushed the file toward them. "Take the file with you. I already had Abe make a copy for our office. Hold on to this as long as you need. If it actually winds up helping you catch the guy and he turns out to be the serial killer, then more power to you. Just be sure to let me know."

"Count on it," Campbell and Liberty said almost in unison.

Chapter 19

It was back.

That same feeling was back.

He could feel it slowly taking over, moving through his body like an all-consuming snake, chewing away at him until there was nothing left but that feeling.

Demanding to be fed.

After the last time, he had honestly thought that he was done with it. That he had reached the very apex of this all-but-draining need to make Sarah pay for what she had done to him. That he had finally conquered her.

But he had been wrong.

That overwhelming need was back. Back and filling up spaces inside him at an incredible, breathtaking speed.

He knew what he had to do.

And soon.

"Where did you get all this information?" Valri asked, skimming through the various notes in the file Liberty and Campbell had brought in for her to look over and review.

"It seems that Benjamin Wallace—our alleged serial killer's real name—had a juvenile record that had somehow slipped his attention. Lucky for us, it managed to fall through the cracks. It never even crossed his mind when he was busy creating his alter ego," Campbell told his cousin.

It was, he thought, like stumbling across a gold mine.

Valri continued searching through all the data. There was a lot to work with.

"Alter ego," she repeated. "You make him sound like a superhero."

"Well, we know that he's far from that," Campbell guaranteed. "If even half the things attributed to him are true, the guy's the devil incarnate," her cousin told her. He indicated the file. "We've brought you all the extraneous information we were able to gather up from that police chief's office. There's even a set of fingerprints on file, not to mention a rather decent mug shot of the guy when they arrested him for some teenage infraction."

It seemed to Valri they had everything they needed to build their case. "And just what is it that you would like from me?" she asked the two detectives.

"Well, in short, can you put all the pieces together and track down this guy's current whereabouts? He seems to be missing," Liberty told the computer tech.

"You mean you want me to close my eyes, wave my hand and presto chango, tell you that he's hiding in the library?" Valri asked whimsically, sarcastic humor curving her mouth.

Campbell saw that his cousin was having fun at their expense, and this was way too important for that. "Something a little more sophisticated than that, Val," Campbell told his cousin.

Liberty broke it down to its simplest components. "What we're really trying to find out is if his likeness appears on any of the current dating sites."

"Dating sites," Valri repeated. It felt as if they had come full circle in their pursuit of this killer. "Do you have *any* idea how many of those things there are out there?" Valri asked them.

"Probably tons," Liberty guessed. If that wasn't the case, they wouldn't have come to Valri in the first place, but she refrained from pointing that out. "Maybe you could narrow it down to ones that focus on strictly professionals. He is preying on nurses, so he needs to focus on an array that would give him his choice. Plus, he likes showing off how smart he is and how exciting a life he leads, working for the FBI—or at least telling these women that's what he does," Liberty qualified. Finished for now, she held her breath then looked at Valri hopefully. "Does that give you anything to work with?"

"As a matter of fact, it does," the other woman replied. It gave her a lot of possibilities to work with. "But, despite anything Cam here—" she nodded toward her cousin "—might have told you, I do not arrive at answers faster than the speed of light. Pinpointing this guy's location is going to take time—if it's even possible," she reminded Liberty. She wanted the woman to be aware of all the drawbacks.

Liberty tried not to look disappointed. Time was the one luxury they didn't have. By all indications, the serial killer had escalated his agenda in the last couple of weeks. Where once he had killed a victim every month or so, in the last two weeks he had killed three women. Whatever was causing him to kill these women, the urge had suddenly, somehow increased, and he was apparently switching tracks.

Campbell squeezed his cousin's shoulder to silently encourage her. He had long ago made peace with the fact that theirs was a touchy-feely kind of family who actually benefited from that silent contact.

"Do what you can," he told Valri.

"I always do," his cousin replied. She looked at Liberty rather than at Campbell when she promised, "And I'll notify you the second I find something for you to go on. In the meantime, try to focus on something else. Better yet, unwind."

Right, Liberty thought. Like that had even a remote chance of happening right now. But in any event, both she and Campbell thanked Valri for her time and for any help that she could give them in their investigation, and then they left.

"I don't know about you," Liberty said to Campbell

as they once more headed down the hallway toward the elevator, "but I'm going to start poring through the various dating sites, starting with the one that Cynthia Ellery was on."

"What makes you think you'll find Wallace under his name?" Campbell asked her.

"I probably won't," she told him, "so I'm just going to go through all the photos of dark-haired, good-looking men presenting themselves as law enforcement agents. Or men claiming to work for the CIA, DEA, or any one of those alphabet agencies."

Campbell looked at her when they reached the elevator. "You think he's good-looking?"

"That's the only thing that he's got going for him. Not good-looking like present company, of course," she told Campbell with a teasing grin as they got on the elevator, "but the man definitely isn't going to stop any clocks—unless, of course, you're basing that on what his soul is capable of."

Campbell inclined his head, giving her the point. "Nice save."

"It's the truth," Liberty replied simply. They were on their way up to the homicide department. "Do you know if there's a free computer in your squad room or conference area?" She was dying to get started in her search of the dating service.

"Yeah, Ed Raffinelli's on medical leave for a week," Campbell recalled, "so his desk is free."

"Sorry to hear that," she said then realized she needed to clarify what she meant. "That he needed to go on medical leave, but not that there's an empty desk for me to use."

Campbell nodded. "His desk's one row away from mine—in case you need anything."

Liberty merely smiled at the information. "I think I'll be able to find you without having to resort to a tracking dog," she told him. And then she grew serious. "Your superior won't mind having me in his office like this?"

Campbell shook his head. "What the lieutenant cares about, first and foremost, is having this case solved and closed. If you can help in any way with that, then you're golden."

"I think I'm going blind," was Liberty's response several hours later when Campbell asked her how she was doing. "I had no idea that there were so many people out there looking to have someone in their lives. It's kind of sad, really," she told him. Of course, she had never been in a position to need someone to complete her—until she had encountered Campbell, she realized. Now she totally understood where those other women were coming from.

"Any luck finding our killer?" Campbell asked.

She looked at the profiles she had printed up. "A few possible candidates, but nothing for sure," she said. "The photos they've posted aren't the best. That is, they are, but they don't look as if they're current."

She looked worn out, he thought. He definitely knew what that was like. "I just finished that report I'd said I would turn in. Since that's out of the way, why don't I join you in going through that dating site you have open, and whatever other site you can think of." Saying that, he thought of something else. "Tell you what, why don't I ask Choi to join us as well. We should be able to pull up a few possible likely suspects between us. Fresh eyes might help."

"Anything you can do to keep me from going cross-eyed will be greatly appreciated," she told him with feeling.

"Can't have you walking into walls now, Arizona. What sort of host would that make me?" he asked with a straight face.

"One who wants to keep his own eyesight," she answered. "The really funny part is that finding this man's so-called 'bio' amid all these various entries is supposedly the easy part. Catching him before he kills again is going to be the really tricky part," she concluded.

"If this guy actually does turn out to be the serial killer," Choi pointed out, joining them when Campbell waved him over. "When you come right down to it, we still haven't pinned that part down yet."

She was well aware of that. She was also very aware of this gut feeling that hadn't abated since they'd found the last buried body. "I'm willing to bet that he's the one."

"And you know this how?" Choi asked, curious if he had missed something.

"Just a gut feeling," she answered, meeting his eyes head-on. She wasn't embarrassed by her convictions. Somehow, it didn't feel as "out there" as it once might have, especially when Choi didn't just laugh at her reasoning.

Instead, the detective looked at his partner and grinned. "Hey, Cam, she's perfect for you. She's got the same kind of sideways thinking as you do," the detective laughed.

Instead of getting annoyed, Campbell merely brushed off his partner's comment by saying, "Haven't you heard great minds think alike?"

"Know what I think? I think you've been dipping into the spiked eggnog a little too much," his partner commented.

"Okay," Liberty declared, "back to work."

Less than twenty-four hours later, thanks to a really concentrated effort on all three of the detectives' parts, they managed to find four different dating websites that boasted photos as well as profiles of four different men. All of whom bore a very striking resemblance to the man the Gainesville police chief's version of a computer tech had tracked down for them.

As expected, each of the men had different names but only slightly different descriptions, backgrounds and careers. But the one thing that remained the same was that each man expressed an interest in finding a woman involved in the medical field. The dating profiles never specified a nurse, but it wasn't all that hard to realize that was what these four different men were all looking for: a woman who was a nurse.

"Okay," Liberty announced, leaning back and

studying all four men—whose photos in her mind were all just slightly different retouches of one and the same guy. "Now I need to come up with a profile that 'Jason Anderson,' 'Jimmy Allen,' 'Jordan Arroyo' and 'Jerry Abernathy' would all be attracted to," she said, wondering if there was any significance in the fact that all the men's initials were J.A.

"I think, with a little bit of makeup wizardry as well as appropriating a new hairstyle, I can get myself to resemble the last couple of victims," she said, more to herself than to either one of the men in the room.

"Okay," Campbell said, not wanting to oppose her, although everything within him was against any of this happening. "I realize you have to bait this trap, but you're not really thinking of turning up on these so-called dates are you?" he asked Liberty.

She looked at him in surprise. Was he kidding? "Well, of course I am. How else are we going to be able to get this guy?"

"By having someone else pretend to be a nurse on the dating site," Campbell said.

That was when it really hit her. Campbell was trying to prevent her from getting the goods on her foster mother's killer. This was the only straightforward way she knew how to accomplish that. "Are we going to have a problem, Cavanaugh?"

"No, no problem, Arizona," he told her, setting his jaw. "Not as long as you listen to me."

Liberty tried another approach, looking at it from his viewpoint. "Look, Campbell, I appreciate your concern, I really do, but nobody—and I mean *nobody*—is closer to this than I am or can do a better job getting the goods on this guy than I can. I have been living and breathing this case for a while now—and it's been eating away at my gut from the moment Florence became a casualty. I *have* to do this," she insisted.

"Why? Because no one else can do it the way you can?" Campbell asked with an underlying mocking tone in his voice.

Liberty raised her chin, looked him unblinkingly straight in the eye and never hesitated in her answer. "Yes."

Choi spoke up then, doing his best to break the tension and lighten the moment. "Look, man, we're all going to be out there, watching her back. This guy's not going to get a chance to hurt so much as a single hair on her head."

Cavanaugh scowled at the imagery. "It's not her hair I'm worried about."

To Liberty's recollection, no one had ever worried about her before. Oh, once she had entrenched herself within the law enforcement structure in Calhoun, she did feel that she wasn't just out there alone as she did her job, but she had never felt like she was being looked after, like someone with a guardian angel looking over her shoulder. She smiled at Campbell and nodded.

"Duly noted and appreciated," Liberty told him and then, with all the conviction she could muster, said, "Okay, gentlemen, now let's see if we can get this SOB so that he never, *ever* hurts a hair on anyone else's head ever again."

She said the words with such feeling that as worried as he was that she was risking her life, Campbell couldn't find it in his heart to try to talk her out of it.

What he did do was resolve to keep her safe at all costs. It was the only way he could see out of this complicated situation.

"Write up your profile and Choi and I will look it over before you post it."

She had thought about going a more direct route. "I just thought I might contact him on the website," she told Campbell. More than anything, she wanted to get this over with as quickly as possible.

"No," Campbell said, vetoing the idea. "Only as a last resort. Otherwise, you might wind up spooking him. He's lasted this long because he's got some pretty keen survival instincts."

"He's right, you know," Choi told her, backing his partner up.

"Yes, I know," Liberty said grudgingly. "That doesn't make it any easier to go along with."

"We could always get someone else to play the part of the nurse," Campbell told her.

She gave the detectives less than a sunny look. "I'm writing it, I'm writing it," she informed them, her fingers flying over the computer keys as she composed her profile.

Campbell only wished that he could feel triumphant over this newest development—but he didn't.

Chapter 20

How did people do it?

Liberty couldn't help wondering that as she shifted in her seat at the restaurant. This was her fourth so-called "date" garnered from almost as many websites in four days.

She was doing it because she was on a mission. But if it wasn't because she was trying to zero in on this sick, cold-blooded killer and bring him down—if she were in this strictly to find someone to share at least part of her life with—she would have definitely felt ready to throw in the towel and call it quits.

Permanently.

How could regular people possibly put themselves through this grueling process? Even playing the part, Liberty was damn tired of putting herself out there, doing her best to look eager and interested every time the door to the trendy restaurant opened and a new customer walked inside.

She had never considered herself an outgoing person, but for the purposes of making this look genuine and, more importantly, to make it work, Liberty had had to transform herself. That meant she had made herself seem like the last word in eagerness when it came to meeting this potential new "candidate" for her attention and, supposedly, her affection.

The truth was, she wouldn't have been caught dead going through all these contortions just to have someone in her life. She had always felt that if it was going to happen, it would happen.

This isn't for you. This is for Florence. Not to mention all those poor women who lost their lives because they had gone looking for love in, as it turns out, all the wrong places.

She blew out a breath, feeling exceptionally uncomfortable as well as impatient.

Scanning the semi-filled establishment, she could see Campbell appearing to share a dinner with a young woman he had earlier introduced to her as his sister, Jacqui. They were talking about something and he looked incredibly serious.

His partner, Choi, was sitting at another table with a female detective who had been recruited for this at the last minute. His previous "date" from the other night had had a family emergency to deal with. There was also another pair of detectives posing as a couple at another nearby table.

These were her reinforcements, Liberty thought. She knew she should feel comforted by their presence.

But when the restaurant door opened and her so-called newest "date" walked in, Liberty felt as if she was very much on her own. Taking a deep breath, she forced a smile to her lips as she watched her date—this time he had called himself Joseph Abbott—scan the immediate area, looking for her.

She knew the moment the man saw her. He smiled broadly.

Depending on her point of view regarding the situation, Liberty had a good feeling/bad feeling about this.

It was him.

She didn't know why she was so certain, but she was. Maybe it was the way he smiled when he saw her. Or the fact that his eyes, even as they took in every inch of her, seemed flat as they washed over her. Flat enough to send a chill down her spine as he made his way toward her.

"Barbara Ellen?" he asked in a deep, baritone voice when he reached her table.

Liberty nodded, responding to the alias she had used on the profile. "Joseph Abbott?" Liberty asked, trying her best to sound pleased to meet him. The man was even better looking in person than she had initially thought he was when she had looked at the photo in his profile. He resembled the others she had gone through on the various dating sites—and yet there was something different about him.

"Guilty as charged," he told her, flashing a bright smile as he slid into the booth and took the seat opposite her. "Am I late?" he questioned, referring to the fact that she had apparently been there for a while.

"No, I'm early," she told him. "I came straight from the hospital because I was afraid I was going to be late. I'm afraid I didn't have time to change." She glanced down at her nurse's uniform. "I hope you don't mind."

"Mind?" he echoed incredulously. "No. As a matter of fact, I have a confession to make." He leaned in a little, as if actually sharing a secret with her. "I've always had a weakness for a woman in a nurse's uniform."

Something in Liberty's stomach tightened just then. She really hoped that nothing in her expression gave her away and tipped him off.

"First time I've ever heard that," Liberty told the man sitting across from her. She found it difficult to contain herself.

The smile on his lips unnerved her. And then he opened his menu. "Have you ordered anything yet?" he asked her.

"No, I thought it would be better if I waited for you," she replied.

"To see if I'd show up?" her "date" asked her knowingly.

So, he was going to play this with a bit of honesty, was he? That freed her up to do the same, she decided. "Well, frankly, yes," she answered.

He almost sounded interested as to her reasons. "Been burned on this route before?"

She weighed her options then admitted, "Once or twice."

"Well," he said magnanimously, "you can put that all behind you." When he spoke, he made it seem as if she was the only one in the room. "If this goes as well as I think it will, you won't have to endure going on those dreaded 'first dates' anymore."

Her eyes met his. She tempered her response with just enough caution. "That sounds promising."

The smiled that claimed every corner of Joseph's mouth seemed almost genuine—until she looked into his flat eyes again. They seemed almost positively reptilian.

"You have no idea," Joseph assured her with just the proper amount of enthusiasm. He nodded toward the menu lying next to her. "Order anything you want. The sky's the limit," he told her loftily, adding, "I want you to look back on this night and feel that *this* was the beginning of the very best part of your life."

Rather than appear to get carried away, she said, "That sounds promising, but I try to keep my expectations low."

"Bad experiences?" Joseph asked with what almost sounded like genuine concern in his voice.

But again, his eyes gave him away, she thought. A concerned person just wouldn't look like that, she told herself.

Still, she murmured, "Something like that," in response to his question.

"Well, I'll do my best to wipe that all away for you," he promised. "Would you like a drink?" Joseph asked as he saw their server approach their table with a basket of warm bread.

"No, thank you. I like keeping a clear head," she said, turning down his offer.

He didn't seem bothered by her refusal. Instead, he nodded. "Very smart of you," he told her then smiled. "I find levelheaded women a definite turn-on."

She knew that the comment was calculated to put her at ease and make her smile. Even so, Liberty could feel herself growing progressively tense.

"I guess that gives us something in common," Liberty acknowledged.

"Good," Joseph declared. "Now let's see what else we have in common," he proposed. Then, out of what seemed like left field, he asked, "What made you want to become a nurse?"

All she had to do was channel Florence and she had her answers, Liberty thought. "I guess I always liked helping people."

"Noble," he commented, nodding his head in approval. The smile on his lips said otherwise.

Heaven help her, it made her skin crawl.

"Not everyone feels that way."

Something in his tone alerted her. "Why, did you have a bad experience with a nurse?"

For a split second, she saw his face darken when she asked that.

She had hit a nerve, Liberty thought, hoping that the others listening in on this exchange had taken note of the way he had paused. She fought the temptation to look in Campbell's direction, but she knew better than to give in to that.

And then Joseph resolved that dilemma for her by saying, "Let's talk about something more pleasant."

He flashed her a bright smile that from where she was sitting seemed to her to be just the tiniest bit stilted and forced.

"I'm certainly all for that," Liberty told the man she was now certain was Benjamin Wallace. "Life's too short to waste with unpleasantries."

For the next forty-five minutes, Liberty found herself caught up in an exchange of some rather aimless banter. Along with the somewhat mind-numbing conversation, she found herself consuming some far tastier offering of lobster bisque.

When the dinner was finished, Liberty's date suggested, "Why don't we go somewhere to top this off?" he said. "I know somewhere that serves great espresso and makes their own out-of-this-world cheesecake. Are you interested?"

Not in the slightest, she answered him silently. But there was no way to prove she was right about this man just going on her gut feeling. No matter how strong it felt to her, she knew she was going to need more than that.

"Sure," she said gamely. "Where did you have in mind?" She hoped the others listening in on her wire were picking this up.

"This little hole-in-the-wall I know of on the outskirts of town. I just stumbled across it," he told her proudly. "My job working with the FBI takes me to all sorts of out-of-the-way places," he told her, raising his hand to get the server's attention. He wanted to pay the bill and get going.

A sense of urgency was pushing him.

"That really sounds fascinating," she all but gushed. The words almost caused her to choke.

She could see that Joseph really absorbed her enthusiasm. "You have no idea," he told her almost smugly.

"What's she doing?" Campbell asked his sister, immediately going on the alert. From where he sat, the man sitting across from Liberty was looking at her like a cat eying a mouse he had picked out for dinner.

"Her job, Cam," Jacqui told him pointedly. "Like it or not, her job."

Campbell frowned, never taking his eyes off the man they suspected of being the serial killer. He didn't like any of this. "We didn't review this part," he all but growled at his sister.

"Maybe she thought it was time to up the stakes a little. Face it, Cam, right now all we have is that the guy bought her dinner. From where we're sitting, that's not exactly an actionable offense," she pointed out. "You can't arrest him for that."

Campbell shot her a look. "Don't talk to me like I'm an idiot."

"Then don't act like one," Jacqui said with a wide smile.

Campbell was on the alert again. "They're leaving," he needlessly told his sister.

She could guess what was going through his head and she felt for him. That didn't change the situation. "She's wired, big brother. We're not going to lose her," she assured him.

He wasn't convinced of that. "I like covering my bets," Campbell told her. "And that *never* involves being too confident," he said with feeling.

"There're six of us," Jacqui calmly reminded her older brother, "not counting Liberty, who struck me as being very competent the one time I met her."

He didn't care what his sister felt, he wasn't about to take any chances. "You know that old saying that anything that can go wrong will go wrong?" he asked Jacqui.

On his feet, Campbell left a twenty and a five on the table to cover their two coffees and desserts, and a little more. He was not about to waste any time waiting for the server to write up their bill.

Making eye contact with Choi, Campbell nodded. His partner and date and the other couple all followed Campbell and his sister out of the restaurant, then circled around to the rear parking lot.

When they got there, they saw that Liberty's car was still parked where she had left it near the rear exit. Liberty, however, even though she had just walked out with her date, was nowhere in sight.

Neither was her date.

Campbell stood there, scanning the area from one

end to the other, searching for some sign of either one of them.

There wasn't any.

"Where the hell is she?" Campbell demanded angrily, his nerves getting the better of him. He could feel his heart all but seizing up in his chest.

Liberty wasn't anywhere around, he thought, his breaths growing shorter and more pronounced with each second that went by.

They looked all around the immediate area. It was Choi who zeroed in on it.

"Cavanaugh, look," he said, calling attention to the object on the ground next to her vehicle's rear right tire.

Campbell was instantly on his knees, picking it up. "It's her phone," he said numbly. Liberty never went anywhere without her phone. He had thought more than once that she was all but glued to it.

This was definitely not good.

"Now what?" Choi asked.

Campbell had always felt that he was equal to any emergency that came up, any unforeseen development, but he had never been personally involved the way he found himself being now.

It was as if his brain had just stopped functioning and he couldn't think.

"I don't know," Campbell answered, his mind going in a hundred different directions at once, searching for a solution and trying to think of what he could do to prevent an irreversible disaster from happening. "Give me a minute to think."

"Well, while you're thinking, I'm calling Valri," Jacqui declared, taking out her cell phone.

The throbbing in Liberty's brain was slowly beginning to subside.

Blinking in the darkness, she tried to make out her surroundings. The lack of any fresh air and the crammed position her body was in told her that somehow, her date must have shoved her into a trunk.

But not *her* trunk.

Attempting to clear her aching head, Liberty tried to piece things together. She recalled walking with Joseph to his car. He had told her that he'd wanted her to see it so that she could more easily follow him to the restaurant he had told her about. The one with the so-called world's best espresso.

Liberty remembered noticing that one of his rear tires had looked just a little flat. He couldn't see it and had said as much, so she'd pointed to it, although she didn't get all that close to it. Even so, Joseph had somehow used the time to pop open his trunk and, rather than take out his spare tire, he'd shoved her inside instead.

It had all happened so fast, she hadn't had time to fight back. Mainly because, before she'd known what he was doing, he had hit the back of her head, knocking her out and, she now assumed, pushed her into the trunk.

Everything had gone black by then. For how long, she had no idea, but she had a feeling that it couldn't have been all that long.

It was hard for her to focus.

Not because of the dark, but because of the throbbing headache that refused to abate or clear up.

She couldn't help wondering if this was what Florence had felt in the final moments of her life. Confused, disoriented, afraid—and horribly violated. Not physically violated. But, as a person, her space had definitely been violated.

Liberty was certain he was preparing to get rid of her the way he had the others. Well, she did not intend to go easily.

She didn't intend to go at all, really, when she came right down to it. She resolved to make this animal pay for every single life he had taken during his hideous spree.

Growing accustomed to the dark, Liberty tried to find something within the trunk she could use as a weapon.

Anything at all.

She focused on what felt like a tire iron tucked into one side of the trunk's interior. Shifting awkwardly, Liberty managed to wrap her fingers around the filthy piece of metal and tugged.

It took her several tries to loosen the tire iron in the space where it had been secured for who knew how long.

Liberty scraped her knuckles in the process and she could feel them bleeding, but finally, she got the tire iron free. It was something she could use to defend herself.

She was not about to go quietly, she vowed, and

if this killer thought that, he was in for one hell of a surprise.

Her breath caught in her throat as she felt the car slowing down and then stopping.

Her hand wrapped around the tire iron, Liberty braced herself for what she knew was going to have to be the fight of her life.

Chapter 21

The moment the trunk lid popped open and Liberty saw Wallace's face leaning in directly over hers, Liberty knew she only had one chance to save herself.

Without even thinking about it, Liberty swung the tire iron she was holding at his head as hard as she could.

She made contact with Wallace's face, specifically his cheekbone, and she managed to smash it. Liberty could hear the bone crack at the same time that Wallace let out a blood-curdling scream of pain and outrage.

Liberty immediately vaulted out of the trunk, simultaneously shoving the man back and away from her with both hands.

She pushed him as hard as she could.

Stunned and caught completely off guard, her would-be assailant stumbled backward, but he still somehow managed to catch himself quickly enough.

"Why you little bitch!" Wallace shrieked angrily at her.

As Liberty started to run away from him, he grabbed her by her hair and held on tightly as he jerked her back. Handfuls of hair were yanked out.

Tears of pain sprang to her eyes and slid down her cheeks. It didn't stop her. She put up one hell of a fight, screaming at the top of her lungs, calling for help.

This wasn't the middle of the night. *Somebody* had to hear her, she desperately reasoned.

Determined to fight him off, Liberty recalled every single defensive move she had ever learned and used. Not just the ones she'd been taught when she'd joined the police force, but ones she had made a point of learning way back when she was being passed from one foster home to another. She'd wanted to be prepared in case someone wanted to get too handsy with her—the way that one kid, the son of the woman who had taken her in, had attempted. She'd lasted at that house for exactly one night, but what she was proudest of was the fact that she hadn't allowed Stephen to touch her.

Liberty had almost managed to get away from Wallace when she suddenly felt her ankle being grabbed. She went down hard as Wallace pulled her, flailing, to him.

Desperate, repulsed and incensed, she twisted around onto her back and kicked Wallace as hard as she could in his manhood with her other leg. That elicited another shriek of pain, followed by a barrage of ugly curses from him.

"You're really going to pay for this," he promised viciously, scrambling to his feet. He chased after her. "Big-time!"

He was going to have to catch her first, Liberty vowed, sprinting from him as fast as she could go. The temperature had dropped and it was cold out, but she was sweating profusely as she raced to get away from the enraged killer.

Because she was unfamiliar with the area, Liberty found herself running blindly down one street.

It turned out to be a dead end.

Wallace was right behind her and quickly managed to close off her avenue of escape. Her back was literally against the wall.

He leered at her, his triumphant air unmistakable. "Looks like your luck ran out. And I promise that you're not going to go easy. You lost that option," he told her with terrifying relish. "I am *really* going to enjoy making you pay, Sarah," he promised the woman who wasn't there.

His eyes all but gleamed with anticipation.

Liberty cast about for something to throw him off balance. She needed to taunt him with the name of the woman it was apparent that he'd been trying to kill over and over again.

"What, a weakling like you?" she laughed, watching his face darken in rage. "You're not man enough. You've *never* been man enough." She began to throw words at him that she was creating on the spur of the moment. "I couldn't beat it into you or discipline you enough to make that happen, although, lord knows I tried. You're just a useless husk of a man." She spat the declarations. "You always have been."

Wallace shrieked, almost blind with fury as he lunged at Liberty.

She ducked down out of the way at the last moment, doubling up her fist and sinking a hard right into the center of his gut.

She had caught him off guard, but she hadn't managed to stop him.

Spitting blood, her assailant wrapped his hands around her throat, murder blazing in his eyes as he began to squeeze.

Hard.

In one quick movement, he had somehow wrapped piano wire around her throat and then begun tightening it more and more.

"I get the last laugh, Sarah!" he crowed happily as well as ominously.

"Think again!" Campbell shouted, bursting into the alley. His gun was aimed dead center at the serial killer's head.

Surprised, the killer didn't release his hold on Liberty. Instead, Wallace shouted almost maniacally, "Don't you understand? She deserves to die! Why won't she stay dead?" he cried.

It was obvious the man intended to carry out what he felt was his mission. Campbell didn't waste any more words on the killer. Instead, he quickly got off two shots, one into each of the man's calves.

Wallace screamed obscenities as he went down, his grip instantly loosening on Liberty's neck.

"'Cuff him!" Campbell yelled back at Choi as he quickly grabbed Liberty's sinking body and pulled her to him. "You're okay, Liberty. You're safe. He's not going to hurt anyone ever again," he promised her as he scooped her up in his arms. "It's over, baby. It's over," he told her over and over again in a calm, soothing voice.

Liberty could barely focus and taking air into her lungs was a huge effort. But she finally managed to get the words out in what sounded like a whisper. "What took you so long?"

Campbell laughed then, irony mingling with a huge wave of relief in his chest. He pressed a kiss to her forehead.

"Traffic," he answered and then called over his shoulder to his sister, "Call two ambulances, Jacqui. One for Arizona and one for this worthless piece of scum." Campbell nodded at the screaming criminal lying on the ground, clutching his wounds and rolling in pain.

"I...don't...need...an...ambulance," Liberty protested weakly. She tried to tug on his arm, but her hand fell without being able to make contact.

"Don't argue with me, Arizona. You're getting checked out," he told the woman in his arms.

"Put...me...down," Liberty ordered him weakly.

"I will. When the ambulance gets here." Looking down at her face, Campbell found he was talking to an unconscious woman.

* * *

Consciousness returned slowly.

When Liberty could finally open her eyes and was able to make out her surroundings, she saw Campbell's face looking far more worried than she would have ever thought he was capable of.

When she could finally speak, her voice sounded as if it was coming from deep inside an echo chamber. "If you're not careful, those wrinkles on your forehead will set in permanently."

Campbell bolted upright. At first, he thought he was just imagining things. He had willed Liberty to speak a dozen times in the last ten hours. At this point, he was afraid to believe his ears.

Moving closer, he clutched her hand and brought it closer to him. Impulsively, he pressed a kiss to her knuckles.

"You're awake," he cried, almost unable to believe it.

"Either that, or we're both having the same dream," she told him then winced. It felt as if the interior of her throat had been scraped with a flaming knife. "I don't think my throat would be hurting like this if I were dreaming," she told him, putting her hand against it to contain the pain.

He felt for her. "No, it wouldn't," he answered. Then he said seriously, "I'm sorry we didn't get there in time. When I think of what could have happened…" His throat all but closed up as the terrible possibilities of what *could* have happened crowded his brain.

Liberty didn't want him dwelling on that. There was no point, and it would only make him suffer. Instead, she focused her thoughts on the positive side.

"How *did* you even find me?" She wanted to know. "That sick bastard took my phone. When I came to in the trunk, I couldn't find it and I *knew* he had to have thrown it. I was certain I was doomed."

Campbell didn't want to tell her that he'd had his own gut feeling about how things could turn out on this mission. Instead he just said, "I like being prepared for all contingencies. That's why in addition to the wire you were wearing, I planted a tracker on you when you went on that first 'date' you arranged on that dating site," he told her.

Liberty didn't understand. "Why didn't you tell me you did that?"

"Simple. Because I didn't want to hear you tell me about how you thought I worried too much or overthought things," he told her.

She was not about to take him to task about that. The pluses of his actions definitely outweighed any possible minuses.

"I'm just glad you did. I don't know how much longer I could have held that monster off," she confessed. "I could literally feel my time running out."

He kissed her forehead, grateful beyond words. "You did better than anyone I know, Arizona," he told her honestly.

"Well, I'm glad for both our sakes that I could surprise you," she said. Sitting up, Liberty told him,

"Now bring me my clothes so I can get out of here. Hospitals make me nervous."

"You can't just leave," he reminded her. "You need to be signed out."

"Then if you care anything at all about me, make it happen, Campbell. I *need* to get out of here so I can focus on the next part," she stressed.

"Next part?" Campbell questioned. "What next part?"

"Getting that bastard to trial so he can be made to pay for what he did," she told Campbell with fierce conviction.

For a moment, he was worried that what she meant by "the next part" was that she was planning on going back to Arizona. Not only wasn't he ready to let her go, he was planning on doing his very best to keep her here. Permanently.

"We'll do it together," he promised her. "But as for now, I'll go get that doctor and *if* he says you can go," Campbell stressed, "I'll take you home."

"No 'if,' Cavanaugh," she told him firmly. "You're taking me home."

Campbell surprised her by meeting her words with a grin. "Oh, yeah, they're definitely going to love you," he said with conviction.

She had no idea what he was talking about. "Excuse me?"

"The family," Campbell explained. And then he backtracked a little. "Uncle Andrew said that the minute you're well enough to be released and up to it, he wants to have that family gathering he mentioned.

This way, you can meet everyone and enjoy a genuine Cavanaugh-style family Christmas."

"But it's not Christmas..." she protested. Then she suddenly looked at him in surprise. "Is it?" she asked, clearly startled.

Just how long had she been out? Was it possible that it hadn't just been a short interval but one that involved the last couple of weeks? She tried to think but she had no way of gauging the time lapse.

"No," Campbell immediately assured her. "It's not Christmas."

"Just how long was I out?" she said.

Campbell was still wearing the same clothes he'd had on when he had brought her to the hospital, but that wasn't really a true gauge of how long she had been there. He might not have gone home to change clothes at any point, choosing to remain at her side.

He seemed like the type, Liberty thought.

She waited for him to give her an answer.

Campbell glanced at his watch. "You've been here ten hours. Long enough to be checked over for any stray bullet wounds and to sleep, not long enough to miss Christmas," he told Liberty. "Now, can I go get that doctor to check you over one last time before he signs you out?"

He expected her to immediately jump at the chance. Instead, Liberty surprised him by saying, "In a minute."

"Okay," he replied, stretching the word out and waiting for her to jump in with an explanation or at least a reason why she was asking him to delay getting the doctor for the moment.

"Campbell?" Liberty said his name hesitantly.

He drew closer to her, looking down into her face. "Yes?" he asked encouragingly, waiting.

"Would you mind just holding me for a minute?" She made the request almost shyly.

This was a side of Liberty that he was definitely not used to or prepared for. He felt as if he were walking a very delicate line playing it light and taking this seriously.

"Well, it'll be hard," he admitted, "but I think I can manage for a little while." Campbell sat on the edge of her bed and gathered Liberty into his arms.

The moment he did, he could feel the tight control she always maintained over herself coming dangerously close to breaking.

And then it did.

The tension of the last four days, not to mention finally coming face to face with the man who had killed so many, who had taken away the life of the only woman Liberty had ever admired, the man who had nearly succeeded in killing *her*—had finally gotten to her.

Campbell knew she had resolved to move heaven and earth to make sure that the man they had caught would be convicted for every single one of those crimes he had committed.

While Liberty was looking forward to the fight, a small part of her felt almost daunted by what lay ahead. She was genuinely afraid in the center of her soul that, somehow, some enterprising defense lawyer would manage to get the worthless piece of scum off on a technicality, and the very possibility frightened the hell out of her.

Liberty sat there in her bed, so many emotons undulating through her. And then Campbell took her back into his arms again.

Maybe it was foolish to think this way. After all, she was first and foremost a realist. But there was something about being in Campbell's arms this way that made her feel totally safe.

She knew she was being irrational, but she didn't really care. All she wanted was to experience the end result of having Campbell hold her. She would deal with the rest of it later.

Much later, but not now.

Chapter 22

Two hours later, after she had been given a clean bill of health by the discharging physician on ER duty and warned to take things easy for a few days, Liberty was lying curled up beside Campbell. It completely amazed her how a place she hadn't even known about less than a month ago now felt like it was her safe haven in more ways than one.

Especially when she was lying in the shelter of Campbell's arms.

They had made love—against his better judgment. Before they'd begun, Campbell had reminded her of the doctor's orders about taking it easy. "Making love," he'd pointed out, "doesn't really come under the heading of 'taking it easy.'"

But she had told him to let her worry about that

and swore that making love with him would do her far more good than harm—unless he didn't want to, she'd qualified at the end.

Since Liberty had worded it that way, Campbell had had no choice but to give in to her, as well as to himself. But he was careful to go slow, which in turn had a beauty all its own.

Now, in the aftermath of the euphoria that wrapped itself around them, Campbell held Liberty to him and softly asked, "Can I get you anything?"

"You already have," Liberty replied, smiling at him. Then, because she could see that he didn't understand her meaning, she whispered, "You."

He kissed her, soundly and with a great deal of affection, not to mention an accompanying huge feeling of relief because nothing had happened to her—and it could have.

Because it wasn't in his nature for Campbell to keep things to himself, he told her, "I don't *ever* want to feel the way I felt today when I thought that I might have lost you."

"What did you feel?" she asked, not to be coy but because she needed to know and trusted him to give her an honest answer. Maybe that made her naive since, up until now, it had never been in her nature to be like this. But this man had made nothing short of a huge difference in her life. And even though she felt that she was being unwise to be so blindly trusting, heaven help her, she was.

"I have never been so scared in my whole life," he

admitted sincerely. "It was like I had a part of myself cut out using a jagged piece of glass."

She winced at the vivid description. "That sounds painful."

"Believe me, it was," he told her. "It felt like nothing short of an eternity until I was able to finally find you." Overcome with emotion, Campbell kissed her again. "You know what I'd like to do?"

She shook her head in response.

"I'd like to put you inside a glass case. But since that's not possible," Campbell went on, "what would you say to marrying me?"

She stared at him, completely stunned. He had just sprung that on her out of the blue without warning.

"You're kidding, right?" Liberty finally asked.

For once, he didn't laugh. "I've never been more serious in my whole life. And," he added before she could say anything in response, "you can ask anyone in the family when you meet them at the party. They'll tell you that I have *never* come close to proposing to anyone."

Liberty laughed softly at that. "Like they wouldn't lie for you."

"Actually, they wouldn't," he replied in all seriousness. "Lying isn't in our DNA. Even for a family member."

"Wow," she marveled, drawing back a little to study his face. "You said all that with a straight face."

Campbell ran his fingertip across her lower lip. "Because I *am* serious," he told her. And then he took her off the hook for now. "You don't have to give me an answer right away. I just want you to think about it." he told her. "Just keep in mind that saying yes would make a *really* great Christmas present for me. You wouldn't have to brave all those crowded stores with their wall-to-wall holiday shoppers," he pointed out as a final selling feature.

Liberty grinned at him. Sometime the man just astounded her, she thought. "You've got it all figured out, don't you?"

Campbell inclined his head. "I do try," he told her.

For now, she focused on something else he had just said. "So you're still taking me to this family gathering of yours?"

"Hey, why wouldn't I? Besides, it's really out of my hands," he conceded. "If I don't show up at the party with you, there's going to be a bounty put on both our heads."

"Well, we wouldn't want that," she said, struggling to keep a straight face.

"Nope, we certainly wouldn't," Campbell agreed.

Just as he drew her back into his arms, his cell phone began to ring. Pausing for a moment to consider his options, Campbell waved his hand at the cell and said something he had never said before.

"I'll just let it go to voicemail."

The next moment, Liberty's cell phone began to ring as well. She sighed. So much for ignoring the call. "I think we need to answer this," she told him, about to pick up her phone.

He frowned, putting his hand on hers. "Let me pick up mine," he volunteered.

Unlocking his phone, Campbell warned the caller, "This had better be good."

"That depends on which side of this thing you're on," the female voice on the other end on the call informed him.

It was Jacqui. If she was calling him at this time of night, he knew it had to be important. He resigned himself to hearing her out.

"It's Jacqui," he told Liberty, glancing in her direction.

"Is Liberty there, too?" his sister questioned. "Good. She's going to want to hear this."

Campbell wasn't sure how to take this. "Hear what?"

"Apparently our serial killer suspect hanged himself in his jail cell tonight shortly after being officially processed," Jacqui informed her brother.

Campbell bolted upright in the bed. "How?"

Startled, anticipating the worst, Liberty asked, "What happened?"

But Jacqui was in the middle of answering his question. Placing the call on speakerphone, Campbell held out his cell phone for Liberty to hear as well.

"Seems that someone at the jail slipped the guy a sheet," Jacqui answered. "Apparently he supposedly made a noose and hanged himself with it." It was obvious that Jacqui had her doubts.

Stunned, Liberty asked in disbelief, "Then he's dead?"

"Deader than a doornail," Jacqui answered. "I'll call you two with more details as I get them," she promised.

Liberty was already throwing off the sheet she had wrapped around her and put her feet on the ground. "Never mind," she said, raising her voice for Jacqui to hear. "We're going there."

Momentarily distracted by what he viewed as Liberty's exquisite body, Campbell had trouble drawing his eyes away from her.

"We are?" he asked.

"We definitely are," Liberty said with conviction. "I want to be able to identify that scum's body and make sure he's dead and not just somehow faking it." It seemed like faking it would be an impossible endeavor, but if it could be done, she knew this maniac could do it.

"You heard the lady," Campbell said into his phone. "We're coming to the morgue."

"I'll meet you there," his sister promised just before the connection went dead.

Chapter 23

Now that it was just the two of them, Campbell had his doubts about taking Liberty with him to the morgue. "Are you absolutely sure you want to go?" he asked Liberty.

She didn't hesitate. "Absolutely. Think of me as a villager," she told him. When Campbell looked at her, confused, she explained, "I need to see proof that the vampire's dead."

He viewed her comment skeptically. "You're not going to ask to see his head mounted on a pike, are you?"

"Don't give me any ideas," Liberty countered as she threw her clothes on quickly.

"You're getting to be really good at that," he said, nodding at her jeans and jersey.

"A girl always needs to build up her skills," Liberty asserted cryptically.

"Personally, I like watching you shed your clothes better," he told her as they left his apartment and headed toward his car.

"One thing at a time, Cavanaugh. One thing at a time," she told him as she got into the vehicle on the passenger side. "Who do you think smuggled in that sheet to that SOB?" she asked, buckling up.

Campbell started up his car and pulled out of the carport. "Any one of a number of people who wanted revenge for a loved one would be my guess."

She rolled the idea over in her mind. "A better revenge would be to see him convicted in a trial."

There was one problem with that, Campbell considered as he drove out of the residential complex. "Yes, but that's leaving things up to chance. Things *can* go wrong in a trial. Hell, he might even be set free. What happened tonight is a far more permanent solution."

His comment caused her to pause for a moment, thinking. "I guess you have a point," she allowed.

Campbell's eyes crinkled as he grinned at her. "I'm a Cavanaugh. I always have a point." And then he looked at her doubtfully again, concerned. "Are you *sure* you're up to this?"

"Even if you have to carry me piggyback on your shoulders," Liberty affirmed.

"Now there's an interesting image," Campbell responded.

Because of the time of night, the roads were all but empty. But it still felt as if getting there took forever to Liberty. She could feel herself almost squirming inside.

It wasn't hard for Campbell to pick up on her tension and impatience. "Almost there."

"There's someone at the morgue now?" she asked him, trying to picture the same situation back in Calhoun. To accommodate them, the medical examiner would have had to come in from a neighboring town.

"There's *always* someone at the morgue," Campbell told her. "Even if it's just a part-time assistant. Don't worry, the place won't be locked up," he said, anticipating what she was thinking. "You'll get to identify the body before sunrise."

"I'm not worried," she told him. "Worse comes to worst, I'll just camp out on the morgue's doorstep until I get to make the identification."

Campbell merely shook his head. She was one incredible, determined woman.

"Well, luckily that won't be necessary because I happen to know someone who has some pull even if the morgue *was* locked."

He was humoring her, and she realized that she probably came across as being too obsessed with this case, she thought as they got out of the car. But one way or another, she needed it to be over. The only way that was going to happen was if she got to view the killer's remains so that she could close this awful chapter once and for all.

"Knew I kept you around for a reason," she quipped with a grin.

"You better have kept me around for more of a reason than that," he informed her, a whimsical smile playing on his lips.

She paused on the top step right before the police station's entrance. Turning to him, she cupped Campbell's cheek with her hand. "Maybe for a couple of reasons."

Because they were totally alone for the moment, Campbell stole a quick kiss. "You're turning my head."

"Just as I intended," she answered.

Liberty was bantering to help relieve the vast amount of tension thrumming through her veins. This was the culmination of what had felt like an interminable quest for her, the hunt for her foster mother's killer, which until recently had felt endless.

Campbell took her arm and guided her into the building even though he knew she didn't need any help. He just did it to let her know, silently, that she wasn't there alone and that he was here for her.

The entrance right before the elevator wasn't as brightly lit as it was during the daytime. But there were still enough lights on to banish the darkness.

They rode down to the basement in silence.

Once again he stopped her just before the entrance to the morgue. When she looked up at him, he asked her for a third time, "Are you *sure* you want to do this? Seeing him this way could haunt you," he warned.

"Not seeing him this way would be worse," she told him. Her mind made up, Liberty pushed open the door and went inside.

The on-call medical examiner appeared half asleep but immediately came to.

"You here to see our latest resident?" the ME asked.

"That's what we're here for," Campbell confirmed. "Would you mind?"

"Not at all. Always glad to close the book on a serial killer," the doctor told them with unmistakable relish. "I heard that this one chalked up quite a body count," he said as he went to one of the drawers that provided a temporary resting place for any of the bodies that were viewed here.

The ME pulled the drawer open. "Here you go," he announced. "Take your time. I don't have anywhere else to be."

Liberty hardly heard the doctor. She had all but slipped into a trance as she stared at the ghostly pale face of the man who had, at last count, created such havoc throughout three different states. One body would have been one too many. Thirty-three or more was completely out of bounds.

But at least now, it was over.

Campbell slipped his hand on her shoulder and gave it a quick, heartening squeeze. "It's finally over," he whispered to her, as if reading her mind.

Her words emerged on a sigh as she stared at the face that had loomed, threateningly, over hers. "Yes, it finally is."

Chapter 24

Liberty thought she knew what to expect when she walked into the former chief of police's house, especially since she had been there for dinner less than three weeks ago. At that time, she had even seen the twelve-foot Christmas tree that, even partially decorated, had taken her breath away.

Or at least, she had assumed that the tree was fully decorated. But when she walked into the chief's house with the unbelievably incredible scents of Christmas Eve dinner wafting in the air all around her, Liberty was nothing short of totally overwhelmed.

And then, without her even realizing it, tears had risen in her eyes.

As had always been his custom, Andrew greeted his visitors at the door. He was about to bestow a warm hug as he told Liberty hello when he stopped short because he saw the tears in her eyes.

Without a word, a handkerchief materialized in his hand, and he silently offered it to her. "But you haven't even tried my Christmas Eve dinner," he pretended to protest. "There's no reason for you to cry yet."

"I'm not reacting to the tempting aromas—which, by the way, smell heavenly," she told him. "I'm reacting to the Christmas tree."

"You don't like it?" Callie, Andrew's oldest daughter asked, disappointed as she came forward to join Liberty and Campbell as well as a few of the other relatives milling about in that area.

"Like it?" Liberty echoed incredulously. "I adore it," she said with enthusiasm. "If *any* version of that tree had ever been part of my childhood, I would have felt as if I had died and gone to heaven." She knew she probably wasn't making any sense to Andrew's family, behaving this way. "I'm sorry," Liberty apologized, at a loss as to what to say as she wiped at her tears. "I'm not usually like this."

Andrew waved away her apology. "Don't give it another thought," he told her, giving her hand a quick, encouraging squeeze. "I find it comforting to find out that underneath that tough exterior is a soft young woman who blends in so well with the rest of us." He then turned toward his nephew. "Campbell, why don't you show Liberty the Christmas decoration that Rose picked out for her to hang on the tree?"

That caught Liberty by surprise. "You have a decoration for *me* to hang?" she asked in disbelief.

"Rose has a great knack for finding just the right decoration for a particular family member. It's a tradition," Andrew told her with a wink.

Liberty was about to protest that she *wasn't* a family member—she hadn't given Campbell an answer—then decided that, just for today, she could pretend that she was. What harm would it do?

"I'd like that," she told the couple with a broad smile.

The next thing she knew, Andrew's wife was handing her a small Christmas ornament box along with an accompanying hook so that she could hang the decoration on the tree.

Liberty felt both nervous and excited as she opened the box, even though she told herself that she was being foolish feeling this way. For heaven's sake, she was a grown woman who had outgrown her need for Christmas and the decorations that went with the particular holiday years ago.

But logic still didn't seem to abate the excitement she felt bubbling up inside of her as she opened the small box.

Her breath caught in her throat when she saw the ornament: a sweet-faced little teddy bear. Liberty found herself blinking back a fresh onslaught of tears. The only thing she had ever wanted as a child was a teddy bear like the one her first foster mother's little girl had had. To her, it had represented a symbol of acceptance.

One she had never felt destined to receive.

"How did you know?" Liberty finally asked, her voice sounding breathless. She had never told anyone about the teddy bear, she thought, mystified. This had to be a coincidence—didn't it?

Andrew's smile told her differently. "Let's just say that I like honing my investigative skills every once in a while," he said with a conspiratorial wink, leaving the explanation at that.

"C'mon, you need to hang it on the tree in order for the ceremony to be official," Campbell urged, taking Liberty by the hand and drawing her over to the Christmas tree. The tree looked completely overloaded at this point.

That was the way she saw it. "There's no room for this," Liberty protested, indicating the decoration in her hand.

"Oh, come on," Campbell said with a laugh then assured her, "There's *always* room for one more." He went on to tell her, "You just have to look hard."

"Get Liberty a ladder," Andrew called out to one of his sons. Then, turning toward Liberty, he explained the procedure. "We always leave the bottom of the tree for the kids to decorate."

"The kids we don't want climbing up on the tree yet," Rose told her.

All in all, like everything else that involved the Cavanaughs, Liberty noted, hanging the decoration—which she had fallen in love with—turned out to be a true family affair. She climbed up on the ladder that had been provided and, after doing a bit of searching, finally found a spot on the tree where she was able to hang her decoration.

"Watch your step," Campbell cautioned as she started to come down.

"I have no intentions of falling," Liberty informed him just a second before her foot slipped on one of the rungs as she descended.

Anticipating a possible fall, Campbell wrapped his hands around her hips to keep her steady as he helped her.

"And *that* is the proper way to come down a ladder," he told her.

Rather than take offense, Liberty caught herself laughing. "Being here with your family is just a continuing education," she couldn't help commenting with a smile.

Her words were met with approval from several different sources. She could feel her insides warming. After all those years of being on the outside looking in, Liberty felt an unmistakable sense of homecoming.

And for however long it would last, she intended to cherish it.

"All right everyone, dinner is severed," Andrew announced several hours after an enjoyable exchange of conversations had taken place.

"Already?" Liberty questioned in surprise.

"What do you mean 'already'?" Campbell questioned. "We've been here for five hours. If Uncle Andrew hadn't put out all those platters of snacks and treats, we would have probably started chewing on one another hours ago." Leaning into her, he confided, "This has always been a very hungry crowd."

Because, as usual, Andrew had invited all the many family members, not to mention family friends, there were several very large tables set up throughout the area, all within shouting distance of one another.

Dinner, as Liberty had expected, turned out to be a very relaxed, very genial affair that once again made her feel that this was the kind of family she had been missing and looking for all of her life.

"Had enough?" Campbell asked, pushing away his own empty plate and leaning back in his chair.

"One more bite and I'm liable to explode," she confessed. Looking at her plate—which wasn't empty—she shook her head. "It's hard to believe I was ever hungry."

He smiled warmly at her. It wasn't over yet. "Well, you've got fifteen minutes for dinner to settle in," Campbell told her.

Liberty looked at him suspiciously. "And then what?"

"And then there's the opening of the presents," he told her as if it were a specific event.

She couldn't be included in that, Liberty thought. She had already gotten her gift—an official Christmas ornament for the family tree. And besides, she thought self-consciously, she hadn't thought there would be any gifts exchanged. She hadn't brought anything with her other than a bottle of wine for the host and hostess.

Thinking it best to state that up front, she protested, “I didn’t bring anything.”

Campbell wasn’t having any of it. “Doesn’t matter,” he told her. “There’re still things under the tree with your name on them.”

“You’re kidding,” she cried, convinced he had to be pulling her leg.

“Well, I know of at least one thing,” he told her. “You can’t hang back, Liberty,” he said as he took her hand and began drawing her into the room with the Christmas tree. “It’s against the rules.”

She was still convinced that Campbell was just teasing her. There were so many of these family members here, she couldn’t possibly have a gift waiting for her as well.

But she also knew it wouldn’t be polite to fight him on this so she went along with it for form’s sake. Besides, she thought that it would be fun taking part in a family tradition, even if it wasn’t her family or even her tradition.

Being a spectator here for the proceedings was good enough for her.

Liberty listened patiently as the cards on the gifts were read aloud and each present was handed to the proper recipient. She enjoyed the whole ceremony and didn’t even realize it at first when her name was said out loud.

“That’s you,” she heard Rose say to her in a stage whisper.

Liberty blinked, surprised. “There has to be some mistake.”

"No, no mistake, dear. It says it right here." Rose pointed to the card for emphasis. "Liberty Lawrence. That's you, right?" Rose asked with a bright, warm smile.

"Yes, but—" Liberty protested, still certain there had to be some mistake.

"Not buts, dear," Rose told her. "Your name, you open it," the woman said simply, holding out the box to her.

Liberty felt utterly self-conscious, but she felt bound to do as her hostess suggested.

With the most careful of movements, Liberty tore the wrapping paper away from the box. Opening it, she found there was another gift-wrapped box inside.

And then another box inside that one.

Until, four boxes later, Liberty had worked her way down to a very small black-velvet box.

Holding her breath, Liberty opened that one as well.

Her breath caught in her throat as silence enveloped the room and the lights on the Christmas tree were caught and imprisoned by the heart-shaped diamond ring inside the box.

Stunned, Liberty immediately looked up at Campbell even as she felt the inside of her mouth grow dry.

"You were serious. The other day, when you proposed, you were serious," she cried, momentarily forgetting that she was saying those words in front of most of his family.

"My dear, by now you should have figured out that Cavanaughs do not fling about proposals like chicken feed in front of chickens," Brian's wife, Lila, told Liberty. And then, in an effort to afford Campbell and Liberty a measure of privacy, Lila announced to the others, "Coffee is being served on the patio. Let's go, people."

Within moments, Liberty found herself alone with Campbell.

"Did you think I was kidding?" he asked her at that point.

Momentarily speechless, Liberty nodded. "I didn't think I would get so lucky twice in one lifetime—to survive a serial killer and to have you actually propose to me—and mean it," she added, feeling as if she was in a trance.

"Oh, Arizona, you have so much to learn," Campbell told her, "and I'm really going to look forward to teaching you—provided you say yes, of course," he qualified.

For the first time in his life, Campbell felt nervous.

But he found he had no reason to be. He saw his answer in her eyes.

"Of course yes," Liberty cried and threw her arms around his neck just before she kissed him—unmindful of the fact that his entire family was looking on from the patio.

Had she noticed, she would have taken it as a sign of things to come—and been incredibly thrilled. Because along with the love of a good man, she finally had the family she had always wanted from the very beginning.

* * * * *

Don't forget previous titles in the Cavanaugh Justice series:

Cavanaugh Justice: The Baby Trail
Cavanaugh in Plain Sight
Cavanaugh Stakeout
Cavanaugh's Missing Person
Cavanaugh Cowboy
Cavanaugh's Secret Delivery

Available now from Harlequin Romantic Suspense!

HARLEQUIN
ROMANTIC SUSPENSE
COWBOY'S VOW TO PROTECT
CARLA CASSIDY
HARLEQUIN
ROMANTIC SUSPENSE
HIS SOLDIER UNDER SIEGE
REGAN BLACK

COMING NEXT MONTH FROM

HARLEQUIN

ROMANTIC SUSPENSE

#2183 UNDERCOVER COLTON

The Coltons of Colorado • by Addison Fox

Sami Evans has long suspected her father may not be entirely aboveboard. So she's not surprised when her one-night stand turns out to be an FBI agent. Dom Colton needs to get closer to Sami's father, but when Dom and Sami fake an engagement, he's realizing his feelings might be more than a cover.

#2184 CAVANAUGH JUSTICE: DEADLY CHASE

Cavanaugh Justice • by Marie Ferrarella

Embittered and broken detective Gabriel Cortland is forced to pair up with an optimistic partner to take down a prolific serial killer—the one who killed Gabriel's pregnant wife. Gabriel is determined to work alone on this, but Shayla Cavanaugh knows how to break down his defenses. But with a killer on the loose, Gabriel's new lease on life may not last very long...

#2185 COLD CASE COWBOY

Cold Case Detectives • by Jennifer Morey

When she finds refuge at his ranch, Indie Deboe struggles with her feelings for Wes McCann. She's lost everything before—to the same killer who could be a threat to both of them now!

#2186 HOTSHOT HERO UNDER FIRE

Hotshot Heroes • by Lisa Childs

Hotshot firefighter/paramedic Owen James is in danger—and not from firefighting. Someone is trying to kill him, and he finds himself falling for the prime suspect!

SPECIAL EXCERPT FROM

HARLEQUIN

ROMANTIC SUSPENSE

Hotshot firefighter-paramedic Owen James is in danger—and not from firefighting. Someone is trying to kill him, and he finds himself falling for the prime suspect!

Read on for a sneak preview of Hotshot Hero Under Fire, *the latest book in Lisa Childs's thrilling Hotshot Heroes miniseries!*

He winced. "Yeah, I remember..."

A smile tugged at the corners of her mouth, pulling up her lips. "Don't go looking for any flowers from me as an apology."

"There's something else I'd rather have from you," he said, and the intensity of his blue-eyed stare had her pulse racing. Then he leaned forward and brushed his mouth across hers.

And shock gripped her so hard, her heart seemed to stop beating for a moment before resuming at a frantic pace. He'd kissed her before, but it still caught her by surprise. Not the kiss so much as the passion that coursed through her. She'd never felt so much desire from just a kiss. And why this man out of all the men she'd dated over the years?

Why Owen James, who'd hurt her in high school with his cruelty? Who hadn't saved her mother?

HRSEXP0422

Why would she be so attracted to him?

It wasn't just because of his flowers and his apology. She'd felt this passion last night before he'd come bearing the roses and his mea culpa.

She'd worried about him yesterday, but just like in high school, she didn't believe it was possible that he really cared about her, that he wanted her. Was he up to something? What did he want from her?

His mouth brushed across hers again. Then his lips nipped at hers, and a gasp escaped her. He deepened the kiss, and she tasted his passion.

He wanted her as badly as she wanted him.

And that was bad…

Very bad.

Because she had a feeling that if she let herself give in to her desire, she would be the one who wound up hurt next…

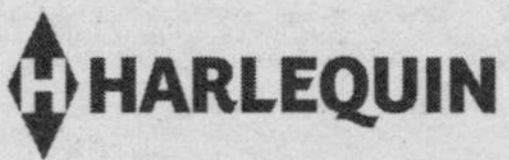
HARLEQUIN